The DAWNING

T0125995

KARIN KALLMAKER

Bella
BOOKS
2009

Copyright© 2009 by Karin Kallmaker

Bella Books, Inc.
P.O. Box 10543
Tallahassee, FL 32302

First Edition, Naiad Press 1999
First Bella Books Edition 2009

Editor: Lila Espon
Cover designer: LA Callaghan

This novel was originally released under the pen name Laura Adams in 1999 by The Naiad Press.

ISBN-10: 1-59493-119-4
ISBN-13: 978-1-59493-119-2

About the Author

The author of more than twenty romances and fantasy-science fiction novels, Karin Kallmaker's repertoire includes the award-winning *Just Like That, Maybe Next Time, Sugar* and *18th & Castro*. Short stories have appeared in anthologies from publishers like Alyson, Bold Strokes, Circlet and Haworth, as well as novellas and short stories with Bella Books. She began her writing career with the venerable Naiad Press and continues with Bella.

Karin's work can be found at www.bellabooks.com. Details and background about her novels and upcoming works can be found at kallmaker.com.

To those who sacrificed
everything
so we could see the stars

Nothing Exists except
by virtue of a disequilibrium,
an Injustice.

All Existence is a theft paid for by other
Existences; no Life flowers except on a Cemetery.

— Rémy de Gourmont

Part 1:
The Injustice

1

Fingers of icy wind found their way into the ancient homes of the Anasazi and trailed across the river where the People's children had played for millennia. The gravelly shore and picnic tables had long been abandoned for winter. The icy touch of the wind sent jack rabbits scampering into their burrows and a lone kinglet flapping home with the last prey it would catch that day.

The spatter of sand against the windows was what had woken me from my fitful doze. As I let the thick, plain curtain fall back into place, I took note of the rattle of distant thunder. I thumped my feet into my hiking boots, added another sweatshirt over the one I had been sleeping in, then shrugged into my black rain slicker. The wind snatched the east-facing door of the hogan from my fingers, and the frigid air scattered playing cards across the floor. I heaved the door shut behind me and set out for the cliff trail Hosteen Sam had shown me long ago.

Trail was an overstatement. I knew every chink and ripple in the domes of deep red rock and the desert-varnished walls. The sandstone of the sloping canyon wall was barely marked in many places, and it contained few finger- and footholds when it became steep enough to call my activity climbing. I'd scrambled up this trail at least four times a week for the last thirteen years.

Halfway to the overlook where I would watch the storm's approach, I was blasted with the first of its true force and nearly lost my grip. As I clung stubbornly to the face of the canyon wall, I could wish that I had fallen, except I was not high enough for a guaranteed fatal tumble. I did not want to lie broken and bleeding when the night predators decided I was tasty. "Come on, Amanda," I said with my cheek against the cold, porous rock. "You're too stringy to be of much interest to coyotes."

After the most strenuous moments of the climb, I swung my leg up onto the ledge and gasped for oxygen in the thin high-country air. The wind whipped my hair into my eyes, and I had to tie the red mess back with the string from my slicker hood.

I turned east to catch the spectacle of the enormous storm front as it swirled southwest from the

Lukachukai Mountains. Another front surged north-west around the Chuskas. The mountains of New Mexico funnel their storms around the border mesas and into Arizona's valleys. From where I huddled, I could see the two roiling fronts merging as if joining forces, then turning their fury on a common enemy below, in this case, Canyon de Chelley. Canyon del Muerto, just to the north, would fare no better.

About three hundred yards east the curtain of rain was already drenching the canyon floor. Arroyos were quickly flooded. Chinle Wash was filling; the runoff had begun. There would be flash flooding along the San Jose River and all over the region. No doubt there had been emergency warnings, but I hadn't turned the radio on for a long, long time. The passage of time mattered little to the sandstone and less to me. As Emerson said, time is a poison.

This was easily one of the largest storms I'd ever witnessed. I'd been watching storms since the first week I'd moved into the hogan. Storms, clouds, mist — I knew them all very well. Last year, or was it the year before, I'd finally taken an interest in clear skies. I'd watch the stars march across the heavens on warm nights, wondering what might be moving beyond my ability to see. Satellites, space stations, shuttles — they were all up there. I didn't want to see them. I'd spent thirteen years trying to escape that memory with very little success.

When I wasn't talking to clouds, I read — some-times a novel, but more often philosophers or re-search. I was looking for an answer, a solution, a way to change what I had done, or at least a good reason — but not an excuse — for why it had happened. Of course, just last night I'd been browsing through Sartre, who said nothing happened for a reason. That philosophy did not comfort me.

The wind was howling over the canyon rim. At sixty-five hundred feet, it makes a sharp, hungry sound like nothing I've heard anywhere else. I clutched my slicker hood and hunkered down. The combined cloud bank was tens of thousands of feet high. It lightened from its nearly black bottom to gray in the middle and snowy white at the top. Above the encroaching front, the sky was the intense hue that I called "high-country blue" in my mind. From my ledge nearly at the top of the canyon wall, I was looking the storm right in the eye. Someone in an airplane looking down would have no idea of the fury that was being unleashed on the ground below.

The hiss of the approaching rain grew louder. I took my last look up at the blue sky above the storm. The white stratocumulus clouds boiled upward as they slammed into a pocket of calmer air that resisted the chaos. White plumes of cloud pierced the blue . . .

. . . I was back in time, watching it happen again. The column of exhaust pierced a shimmering blue sky as the shuttle arced higher. *T plus 28 seconds, ten thousand feet.* The shuttle rolled to face earth for ascent attitude. *T plus 1 minutes 2 seconds, thirty-five thousand feet.* Like everyone else, I cheered and applauded. At T plus 1 minute 10 seconds, there was a brilliant flash. Tick, tock, tick. Then where there had been only one column of exhaust there were now two, peeling away from each other as chunks of the orbiter careened in all directions. The crew cabin was falling over a hundred thousand feet, nearly twenty miles down to the Atlantic. They had no ejection capability, and they knew they were falling.

Judy Resnik turned on her oxygen while they fell. NASA was the first place she had ever been where she wasn't the smartest person there, and that had been a welcome change. What never changed was reporters asking a doctorate in electrical engineering and a fellow in biomedical research how she kept her hair coifed in space.

Dick Scobee was commanding a space shuttle because he'd chosen to fly heavy, workhorse aircraft, though his credentials would have let him pick the coveted top gun type training. His people, cargo and craft were flown as if they were made of eggs, but no amount of skill or training can change what happens when flame meets liquid fuel.

Ellison Onizuka grew up in the Kona coffee fields of Hawaii and dreamed of becoming a test pilot. He was the first American of Hawaiian descent in space. On this journey, he had thought he would see Halley's comet and hoped he could find the words to describe it to his children.

Mike Smith learned to fly when he was in high school and chose the Navy over the Air Force because flying off of aircraft carriers was something he wanted to try. When the opportunity to get on the track to admiral had been presented, he'd swerved to the space program so he could keep flying. His voice was the last recorded.

Ron McNair played the saxophone well enough to be slated to record with Jean-Michael Jarre, who would later honor his dead friend with "Rendezvous." He was a black belt in karate and the kind of captain of the football team who tucked books on thermo-dynamics into his gym bag. That is, when he could find them at the branch of the South Carolina library where colored folks were permitted.

Greg Jarvis worked for Hughes Aircraft. Though he'd been in the Air Force earlier in life, he'd spent the last thirteen years designing communications networks, then satellites, for geosynchronous orbit. His wife had begged him to stow her away in a locker so she could share the experience with him, just as they had shared countless bicycle journeys all over the country. He'd been scheduled for deployment and experiments on two other trips, but politicians had bumped him into the seat where he would die.

Christa McAuliffe was the embodiment of what everyone wants schoolteachers to be. She'd overcome a childhood fraught with illness to reach out for the stars in hopes of giving the "Ultimate Field Trip" to the world's children. The children were watching when a fireball hid the orbiter from sight.

They were all falling at two hundred and seven miles per hour. For two minutes and forty-five seconds they all knew they were going to die, and I had helped to kill them.

I didn't realize I had lost my balance until the rock ledge slammed the breath out of me. The wind had pushed me back from the edge and from what would certainly have been a fatal accident. I should have let myself go. It would be fitting, plunging to my own death while reliving the deaths of the seven people I had helped kill. My life really would have flashed before my eyes.

But death wouldn't change anything — I will be

what I am even after I cease to be. Some parts of Sartre do stick with me.

Hosteen Sam said that I thought too much. He'd said the same of my grandmother, who had run a Christian school on the reservation next to the church where my grandfather had preached.

Little Red, he'd said, life is about the crack of light between two abysses.

Little Red, he'd said, hiding in the dark does not mean there is no light.

Little Red, he'd said, lighten up.

He'd delivered these wise words with a bit of Blessing Way song and a dash of cornmeal on my nose. It wasn't until much later that I'd realized the old reprobate had quoted Nabokov at me. Wise is wise, he would have explained. What matters if the wisdom comes from off the reservation? It was impossible to argue with Hosteen Sam. All I knew was that I had squandered my little bit of light.

I clung to the ledge until the first rain stung my cheeks. The vertigo dissipated, and I pulled my hood back over my uncombed hair. The water was rising. No one would be able to reach my hogan for several days — not that I cared. I had visitors once every blue moon, and that was too often.

The murky, copper-color water would rise enough to touch the drooping branches of cottonwood trees waiting for their first blossoms. The rivulets would grow to fast-running streams that would pour down the swirling canyon walls carrying gravel and sand into Chinle Wash, which would, in turn, cover the canyon floor. I watched the rising flood slowly crest a rock I judged to be between two and three feet high.

The pounding of the rain grew even more rapid, like war drums signaling soldiers that now was the time to strike.

From the corner of my perch, I saw a flash of silver. As I turned my head sharply, a roar distinct from the flood and rain rumbled through the canyon. It sounded like a rock fall or an earthquake.

As suddenly as the noise began it stopped. I shook my head, looked again. Standing in the general area where I had thought I'd seen the flash of light was a woman in bright blue all-weather gear. She wobbled on the boulder, then went backward into icy, three-foot floodwater.

I began a hasty slither down the canyon wall. If the woman was swept around the next bend, she wouldn't be prepared for what was now a waterfall. The pressure would pummel her into a series of rocks. If she was pulled toward my side of the wash, there was higher ground where we could both scramble to safety.

Flickers of lightning made me stop halfway down. I shook the water out of my eyes and looked over my shoulder. The woman was clinging to some stubborn scrub. Thunder rumbled from up canyon, and the pounding of the rain became a steady roar. The wash level rose another few inches in a matter of moments. If the downpour didn't let up, it could easily be four feet deep and running fast by the time I waded into it.

Almost at the bottom, I jumped the rest of the way. Bad decision. My boots slipped in the moving gravel and water, and I fell heavily. I struggled to breathe in while I shook away the stars dancing in front of my eyes. When I could see again, there was no sign of the woman. The scrub she had been clinging to was snapped off.

I knew the wash, and that was my only advantage. I sucked in my breath as I plunged into the icy water. It was still shallow enough to wade, but I moved much faster if I let the water carry me. My boots protected me from the boulders, and I had enough leverage to keep myself to the less treacherous side of the wash. I was covering ground quickly, but already the freezing water was making me numb.

There was no sign of the woman. I started to panic — I couldn't let her drown. I could not bear to watch another person die. Not again. I braced myself for rounding the sharp turn and the inevitable cascade on the other side.

The dry pour-off I could usually step down was now a five-foot waterfall. I was moving so fast I catapulted free of the water. The woman had already made it to the safe side of the wash. She turned at my cry and, to my horror, my boots caught her in the stomach. In a tangle of arms and legs, we both plunged into the water again. Fabric brushed past my fingertips and I seized it desperately, then I slammed into a boulder. Something in my left leg snapped.

I was no longer the rescuer. The woman was steadfastly pulling me to the shallow edge of the wash. I swallowed one mouthful of the muddy water, then another went into my aching lungs. The woman yanked me onto the higher ground, then collapsed next to me.

I had just enough strength to lift my face out of a puddle. I spit out a disgusting mouthful of sand and mud, then hacked up what I had inhaled. Just when the spasms in my lungs eased, I vomited up the water

I had swallowed. With every movement bones in my left leg grated and the fiery shocks of pain made me feel faint.

After a minute, the woman rolled me over. All I saw through a haze of pain was a smile, as if the experience had been one grand lark.

"You fucking moron," I spluttered. I tried to sit up, but my leg shrieked agony. We had both been on the way to meet our ancestors, and the woman was still smiling. I wanted to smack her, but I just lay there, breathing hard, while rain pelted into my eyes.

"You are hurt." The woman bent to examine my leg.

"No shit, Sherlock! Goddamn tourists — you have no right to be here!" I could barely speak loud enough to be heard over the drumming rain.

"I can help." Her voice was hoarse, as if she was recovering from a bad cold.

"What? Are you going to carry me into Chinle? It's only twelve miles, most of which is now under fucking water."

"Be calm." The touch of the woman's hand on my forehead was like a wave of Valium. For several minutes I could not move and my injured leg felt hot, almost burning. Abruptly the sensation ended, and I shuddered as the cold rain and water shocked me back to awareness. What the hell had just happened?

"Stand."

I found myself on my feet. My leg wasn't broken after all. I hesitantly put my weight on it, then couldn't help but give the woman a wide-eyed stare. Even the deep bruising I'd incurred when I'd first fallen into the water was gone. I wanted to ask what had happened, but the downpour made conversation difficult. There was time for questions later, after I managed to get some warmth back into my body.

"The house is this way." I scrabbled out of the wash, then led the way. A quarter-mile of slogging brought us to the hogan door. I kicked off my boots just inside the door and heard my companion do the same.

We were covered with mud and sand. Walking had shaken off the cold, but I wanted nothing more than to get clean and warm. I stoked the stove and kicked on the propane-powered room heater. I would never be more grateful for the little water heater that brought the bath temperature up to tepid.

"You first," I snapped. The woman had been watching calmly from just inside the door. "Never let it be said I'm a bad hostess."

The woman said nothing, but stepped behind the curtain to shed her clothes. I averted my eyes and reached in for the sodden clothing, then rinsed the full-length suit as best I could. As I hung it on the line behind the stove, I could tell the waterproof pockets were full of something. I hoped it was the means to get this idiotic tourist out of my life as soon as possible.

When I heard the tub water draining, I left the comfort of huddling next to the room heater. I passed a towel around the curtain and put the coffeepot on to boil. I stripped out of my own filthy clothes and tossed them into the sink for rinsing, then wrapped myself in my robe. When the woman stepped around the curtain wrapped in the towel, I gestured at the dresser. A quick glance told me that, free of mud, she was thin, white and middle-aged. More than that I didn't care to know.

"There are some clothes in there. Help yourself."
The gritty, lukewarm bathwater was as good as a spa.
I felt warmth return to my toes. Even my ears lost
the chill. I scrubbed my hair with the bar of soap and
went under to rinse. It had been a while since I'd
bathed, anyway.

As I toweled off my now uninjured leg, I examined
it for any sign of the damage I knew I had felt. It was
unmarked in any way. Frowning, I ran my hand over
it. Something wasn't right. Then I realized that the
scar from knee surgery in high school was gone. My
fingers trembled with amazement as I brushed the
smooth skin.

I sat back in the water. I wished I had one of
Hosteen Sam's charms against, well, against I didn't
know what. Just whom had I brought into my one
place of refuge? I couldn't doubt the evidence of my
eyes, and neither could I imagine any reasonable
explanation.

I was not going to consider unreasonable
explanations either. This dark-haired white woman was
not some sort of magic healer. I was not in the
presence of an angel. I would sooner believe I had
imagined the knee surgery and the scar than consider
impossible mystic alternatives.

I scrubbed myself dry while my thoughts turned in
circles. I had been denied answers to so many
questions, but exactly how the woman had done what
she had done was going to get answered.

I wrapped my robe tightly, then stepped out to
confront her. She was wearing my Princeton sweats
with her hair wrapped in the towel, and she had one
of my research books in her hand. "I have to know
what you did to me."

There was a brilliant flash of light, then a roar like the sound of an avalanche or an earthquake.

:No, you don't.:

The dry pour-off I could usually step down was now a five-foot waterfall. I was moving so fast I catapulted free of the water. The woman had made it to the safe side of the wash and was already turning to help. I narrowly missed knocking her back into the water. Strong hands seized my jacket and pulled me into the shallow edge of the wash. I swallowed one mouthful of the muddy water, then another went into my aching lungs. The woman yanked me onto the higher ground, then collapsed next to me.

I had just enough strength to lift my face out of a puddle. I spit out a disgusting mouthful of sand and mud, then hacked up what I had inhaled. Just when the spasms in my lungs eased, I vomited up the water I had swallowed.

After a minute, the woman rolled me over. All I saw was a smile, as if the experience had been one grand lark.

"You fucking moron," I spluttered. We had both been on the way to meet our ancestors, and the woman was still smiling. I swung as hard as I could. She evaded the punch, but lost her balance and went down on her butt in a puddle, which served her right. My hip ached with bruises, and rain pelted into my eyes.

"I didn't expect that," the woman said. Her voice was hoarse, as if she was recovering from a bad cold.

"What the hell did you expect? Goddamn tourists

— you have no right to be here!" I wanted to take another swing at her in the worst way. She'd nearly killed us both. I did not help as the woman scrambled to her feet.

"I'm sorry." She didn't look in the least bit sorry to me.

"Like that means a damn. I suppose you want me to show you how to get out of here." What a total fucking inconvenience this woman was going to be.

"If you could help me get oriented, I can find my own way."

"I have a map at home." I scrabbled out of the wash, then led the way. A quarter-mile of slogging brought us to the hogan door. I kicked off my boots just inside the door and heard my companion do the same.

We were covered with mud and sand. Walking had shaken off the cold, but I wanted nothing more than to get clean and warm. I had been planning to show her the maps and send her on her way, but no matter how stupid she was, she didn't deserve to freeze to death. My experience with the weather told me the rain was just a prelude. At this altitude, spring usually announced itself with a good snowstorm.

I stoked the stove and kicked on the propane-powered room heater. I would never be more grateful for the little water heater that brought the bath temperature up to tepid.

"You first," I snapped. The woman had been watching calmly from the doorway. "Never let it be said I'm a bad hostess."

The woman said nothing, but stepped behind the curtain to shed her clothes. I averted my eyes and reached in for the sodden clothing, then rinsed the gear as best I could. As I hung it on the line behind the stove, I could tell the waterproof pockets were full of something. I hoped it was the means to get this idiotic tourist out of my life as soon as possible.

When I heard the tub water draining, I left the comfort of huddling next to the room heater. I passed a towel around the curtain and put the coffeepot on to boil. I stripped out of my own filthy clothes and tossed them into the sink for rinsing, then wrapped myself in my robe. When the woman stepped around the curtain wrapped in the towel, I gestured at the dresser.

"There are some clothes in there. Help yourself." The gritty, lukewarm bathwater was as good as a spa. I felt warmth return to my toes. Even my ears lost the chill. I scrubbed my hair with the bar of soap and went under to rinse. It had been a while since I'd bathed, anyway.

As I was toweling off, I took in the enormity of having a stranger in my place of refuge. I'd come here to hide from the past and from myself. Another person in the small space would be impossible to ignore. I didn't want to explain the way I lived or feel obligated to show interest in whatever her story might be.

"If you could just let me look at a map of this area, I'll be on my way," the woman said as I pulled back the curtain. She was wearing my favorite very faded and very old Princeton sweats.

I moved to the kitchen so that a small counter separated us. I poured two boiling cups of this morning's coffee into the only two mugs I had, then finally glanced at her. She was looking at the books that jammed the shelves along the west wall. From the back, I could tell she was thin, white and middle-aged. More than that I didn't care to know.

17

I had trouble keeping resentment out of my voice. "The rain has let up, but all of the trails will be flooded out for at least a day. It'll be full dark soon." An inner sense was warning me to keep my distance, but I had to leave the kitchen area to give her the mug. "Did you get separated from the rest of your group?"

"No, I'm on my own." She turned to face me, but I refused to make eye contact.

"Then you're in violation of Navajo law," I said haughtily. "You must be accompanied by a Navajo guide to be this far back in the canyon." Typical ignorant tourist.

"I didn't know that. I intended no disrespect. If you could just help me discover where I am exactly, I can find my way to where I need to go."

"Where's that?" I grimaced at the coffee to avoid looking at my guest any more than I already had. I don't like to look at people. Hosteen Sam says that is because I am afraid they will look at me.

"Los Angeles."

I squelched the foreign sensation of amusement and sipped again. It was bad, even by my very low standards. Maybe it was yesterday's coffee. Had I made coffee any time today? I couldn't remember. "Lady, you're a fucking long way from Los Angeles."

"How far is a fucking long way?"

Suspicion that I was being mocked made me look up. The woman's face was in profile as she busily untangled her long, curly, brown hair with her fingers.

I blinked. My mind assembled a whole face based on the half I could see. It was a face I knew from dreams and nightmares.

Sharon Christa McAuliffe, schoolteacher, space shuttle payload specialist, born 1948, died 1986, turned her head and looked directly into my eyes.

I fainted.

2

I heard voices, like whispers of wind, like feathers in my head.

:electromagnetic magnitude . . . what to do . . . she knows about it . . . no . . . bad luck . . . I need to know more . . . abort . . . I can fix it again . . . no . . .:

The voices twined, merged and faded like a distant radio signal. Sometimes there was only one voice, but it always sounded like it was arguing.

Abruptly, silence.

I took a deep breath. I was on the floor. I was

cold. I made the monumental effort it took to open my eyes, but before I could focus, the voice came back.

:Take me to that time. Let me see it as you saw it.:

What time could the voice mean? When I realized what it wanted, I struggled to wake up, but I was already falling back into the past, becoming a person who no longer existed.

I could feel the icy wind on my cheeks as I stood that day at the top of the Capitol steps to admire the reflecting pool, the Washington Monument and the long frost-covered stretch of the Mall. I hadn't worked there long enough to grow tired of it. Even in the subfreezing winter weather I took the surface route between the Capitol and the House Office Building. I wrapped my scarf over my nose and mouth and skipped down the steps.

I remembered it all vividly. As I had passed the Library of Congress, I had promised myself that that night after work I would go inside for the first time. The frigid air felt good in my lungs as I crossed Independence Avenue and went into the stale warmth of the building where Congressman Bill Nelson, D-Florida, had offices.

I knew that it was more than my Princeton grades and extracurricular activities that had finally brought me this plum job in a congressman's office. I was a white girl raised by a Baptist preacher, educated in part at a Christian college and raised in full on the Navajo Reservation. I was assumed to be fully supportive of the Moral Majority agenda that was sweeping through Congress, including the southern

Democrats, and I could supply perspective on Federal-Tribal relations without automatically being thought a biased native activist.

I was not responsible for their assumptions. Hosteen Sam —

:Show me.:

I thought of Sam Nakai. I called him *Hosteen*, which is both a title of respect and a substitute for *Grandfather*. He had steadied my first steps and had always been there when I needed advice. He would stop for coffee and cookies on Saturday mornings, passing the news and some thoughts with my grandmother while my grandfather was writing the next day's sermon. I had always been a little frightened by my grandfather, but never by Hosteen Sam.

He was my grandfather-by-choice and, since the death of both my grandparents, the only family I chose. When I had told him I wanted to take an internship in the nation's capital to learn firsthand how the legislative process worked, he agreed that it might help me toward my specialty in tribal law.

He'd also warned me about forked-tongued men with two hearts. When I had unpacked I found that he had tucked my old kachina into one of my bags. To a Navajo, unlike their Hopi neighbors, a kachina is just a doll. But he knew that to me, the kachina was security. Underneath the doll, there was a small pouch of *tadidiin* — holy pollen. To Hosteen Sam, that was security.

I worked in Congressman Nelson's office because my mid-term graduation had put me in the job market early and my own congressman didn't have a place for me until June. At that time, I was going to be assigned as a very junior aide on tribal affairs. In the interim, Congressman Nelson had paid back a marker by giving me a temporary job in his office. I had started several weeks ago, just before Christmas. The office had been very slow, with most of the activity coming from the district office in Florida. They were occupied nonstop with publicity and media relations for the congressman's space shuttle flight.

Still, the D.C. office found useful work for me reviewing and summarizing a proposed modification of Federal-Tribal land and water use agreement with the Seminole tribe in the congressman's home state of Florida. Since I had finished that, I'd spent a lot of time gofering papers around the capital from the office to wherever the Congressman or his chief-of-staff happened to be now that congress was back in session.

My memories were so detailed. I recalled where the marble floor was cracked, where desks were marked with water stains. I could see the office just as I had entered it that day. I smelled the overheated coffee and heard the background whir of the copier.

More vividly than when I had actually been there, I saw the huge picture of Space Shuttle *Columbia* behind the receptionist's desk. Bill Nelson had spent six days in space during shuttle mission 61-C, an experience he told everyone was one the Lord meant him to have. For a while it had appeared he wouldn't get into space — *Columbia* had been delayed four times over two months, cramping the already ambitious shuttle flight schedule. Since his return from space, Nelson had been on fire to get more money for the shuttle program. He wanted to go back.

The space program and NASA were more than ever Bill Nelson's baby. He chaired the House Space Science and Applications subcommittee that formulated

NASA's budget. That position had allowed him to get his seat on the 61-C mission only two months before its scheduled launch. Senator Garn held a similar position on the other side of congress and had similarly spent his stint in space.

The familiar bitterness seared through me. Greg Jarvis had been slated for Nelson's flight. He'd also been slated for the one Garn had gone on. But no, the politicians wanted their seats according to their schedules, and he had to wait. Jarvis had ended up on the *Challenger* 51-L mission. The launch was now scheduled to fly in two days, on Super Bowl Sunday.

Don't make me do this. I didn't know who I was begging, but someone was forcing me here, to these memories. I couldn't bear it again, not at this intensity. I was living through each minute, but this time I knew what was going to happen. I lived through it in my nightmares, but I wasn't asleep this time. Or was I?

It had been a while since I'd thought about how Nelson and Garn had been tolerated by NASA for purely political reasons and that anyone could have done their part in their missions. It was so obvious the shuttle trip had been *quid pro quo* for Nelson that it had damaged NASA's integrity — that would all come out in the investigations. Later in the year they even had a Saudi prince scheduled as a passenger. It wasn't fair that Greg Jarvis had ended up in that seat.

None of it was fair.

For purely political reasons, to demonstrate their support of education, the Reagan administration had pushed for a teacher in space. The concept had fired people's support for space exploration again. All the networks were going to cover McAuliffe's liftoff; only CNN had cared about Nelson's. That kind of irony was what Hosteen Sam called Coyote's way of rewarding ambition. Nelson had been cheated of the best publicity, but he was alive, I thought, and two children had grown up without a mother, a mother who had died before their very eyes.

Nelson's private secretary was stowing the sheaf of papers she'd brought out with her in the locking file cabinet behind her desk. "I'm glad you're back," she said without any preamble. "Jerry and Tom need someone to take notes."

I left my coat and scarf on my chair and took a yellow lined tablet into Tom's office. Tom was an official aide with some seniority, although he was only a year or two older than I was. He and Jerry were talking Super Bowl when I entered. Neither of them had anything resembling a writing implement within reach. I could remember how much that peeved me. They were little men playing big chiefs.

"Oh good, just what we need," Tom said. His cologne was always too strong. All at once, I had the sensation of being rocketed upward as if in a high-speed elevator. I could feel the cold floor under my back, and I wanted to sneeze.

:*All is well. Take me there again.*:

The urge to sneeze passed, and I fell down the well of memory. I poised my pen over the pad. If they were going to treat me like a secretary, then I would act like one.

"Bill needs some quick points to send down to the Cape about the 51-L launch. The long-range weather is suggesting that *Challenger*'s liftoff is going to be postponed over the weekend. They're going to miss all that Super Bowl publicity. If they're not off the ground by Monday, the mission is scrubbed until summer, and no one on either side of the aisle wants that. Bill wants to make sure the President can remind everyone how important the shuttle program is during the State of the Union on Tuesday night. He even sent Pat Buchanan some language for the speech to augment what NASA sent."

Every minute I relived made me recall ever more vividly the way I had felt that day. I had been surprised that Tom wanted to ensure that Republican Reagan got his PR moment during the State of the Union. I had been tempted to say what everyone in the office pointedly ignored — Nelson's mission had been postponed four times, pushing the *Challenger* mission back month after month. I'd said nothing and I'd felt powerless, as if nothing I could do would have any effect on the shuttle program.

Jerry was nodding solemnly. "The *Challenger* has got to go up by Monday and NASA needs to be reminded that the importance of the citizen missions is paramount to other concerns."

"All the usual points," Tom said, waving at my notepad. "The agency needs to maximize the publicity of the first teacher in space. The public is losing interest in the shuttle program. Taxpayers are reluctant to see their dollars wasted on scrubbed missions. That sort of thing."

I scribbled in longhand. They obviously meant for me to write it out properly. I felt the bad temper in me as I thought about my six years of college, my law program and wasting it taking notes. I would show them I had a brain. "Do you want to end with a reminder about the appropriations conference in mid-

February? Something along the lines of the 51-L mission will be over by then so the conference can focus fully on new appropriations for the space station NASA wants support on?"

Jerry gave me a more respectful look than he had to date. I think he might have seen me as a person for the first time. What a waste. Was that what I had done it for? For the respect of people I didn't respect?

Don't make me do this. I was begging again.

There was another wave of pressure. *:As you saw it, show me.:*

Tom said, with an evil chuckle, "Well that might be effective. Not that it's a threat. Just a reminder."

I said dryly, "Of course not." I was clearly dismissed, so I grabbed the five minutes at the word processor it took to type up a draft and gave the result to Tom. I didn't hear back from him until after another trip over to the Capitol with papers.

"This is ready for signature," Tom said. He put the memo on my desk. The secretary must have done the final because it was properly formatted on congressional memorandum paper.

"I just got back." The sun was starting to set, and it was bitterly cold out now.

"It needs to go tonight," Tom said. "Have a good weekend." End of discussion for him. I have often wondered if he realized he had some responsibility in what would later unfold. Not that it mitigated mine. They were my words, not his.

I glanced at my watch. If I used the underground passage I could be there and back at the fax machine in twenty-five minutes. It would still give me an hour at the Library of Congress.

I dashed through the underground access, darting

around senators and bigwigs from the administration. I lost time when I had to stop moving while Vice President Bush came through, and I tried to make it up by half running. Everyone seemed to be in a hurry, and no one paid me any attention.

Bill Nelson signed the memo after glancing at it only briefly. Back in the office, I dropped the memo into the facsimile machine. After hundreds of years of government without fax machines, everyone now factored the instant communication into their way of doing business.

I watched every move I made in slow motion. I tried to stop my fingers as I punched in the phone number for the NASA administrator's fax machine. Stop, please stop . . . my head was throbbing, but the flow of memory halted.

:Let it go.:

No, I swore. I can stop it from happening, let me stop it.

:Let it go!:

Something shook me physically, and my concentration was broken. In horror, I watched myself push the start button. The paper fed through, and the machine printed a transmission receipt on the odd, coated paper. I put both pieces of paper on my desk. It was done. I'd done it again.

I could sense my own exhaustion, but then a soothing warmth went through me. I was still afraid, but it seemed easier now to do as I'd been bidden — I just let it go, all of it.

The Library of Congress was both worn down and grand. The mural on the vaulted ceiling was beautiful, but the carpet showed the passage of many feet. Banisters were intricately carved, but rubbed free of stain and lacquer. The heavy smell of books and bodies and copier ozone permeated the air. I fished in my satchel for my tribal ID and used it to get access to archival materials on Federal-Navajo relations. The archives were well organized, and most of the historic papers were in protective pouches. I could not wait to write Hosteen Sam that I had touched papers that described his ancestors and their words.

When I came to a dispassionate progress report written by Kit Carson in 1864, I held it in my hands and willed myself not to let the anger I felt toward him give me what Hosteen Sam called bad medicine. The past could not be changed. At that moment, I had thought that I understood wanting to change the past, but I hadn't. I had learned the gnawing desire and the ultimate despair that comes with it a few days later and relived it almost every day for the last thirteen years.

Carson had described in glowing terms the lack of casualties during the Army's Navajo campaign that waged war not on the Navajo, but on their livestock and crops. Starvation led to surrender. Those who didn't surrender were massacred deep in the canyon I now lived in. A later report from Carson touched only briefly on the "insignificant" loss of life while the captured Navajo people were compelled to walk four hundred miles to a dry, barren area unsuited for farming. Their pitiful condition made them perfect targets for other tribes in the area. A camp commander from Fort Sumner wrote that the Navajo brought only disease and starvation, were incompetent farmers, and ought to be sent back from whence they came. Of the eight thousand originally captured four years earlier, slightly more than two thousand walked home again to reclaim a fraction of their lands and rebuild their way of life. The lands they reclaimed turned out to have huge natural gas and uranium deposits on them, which the government paid a pretty penny for. Coyote irony again.

Flickering lights signaled closing time. I put the documents away. I'd been told stories of the Long Walk almost as often as I'd heard my grandfather preach about Christ. When I had told Hosteen Sam how fervently I wished I could go back and make Carson give up the idea of the Long Walk, his answer had been typical of him. "Can you change the wind? But for the wind there could be no corn, no canyon and no Little Red wasting her time in the past."

As I was leaving, I literally ran into a woman who worked in the office next to Nelson's. We both dropped our satchels then we bumped heads as we bent to pick them up.

"Sorry," we said in unison.

"I'm Laney." She stuck out her hand.

Her warm palm made mine tingle. "Amanda. You work next door to me."

"I thought I'd seen you around." It was more than thought. We'd been glancing at each other in the elevator and hallways ever since I'd started working in the building. "They're closing, aren't they? Damn. Well, I can come back on Monday." She had pretty blue eyes and a nose that was slightly crooked. She was looking at me as if she liked what she saw. "Want to go get some coffee?"

It would have taken me weeks to get up enough courage to ask that question. Women together is not that unusual or frowned upon in Navajo life, but I knew full well what my fundamentalist grandfather and the rest of the world thought.

As if to confirm what she meant, she added, "We can take the Metro up to DuPont Circle." DuPont Circle was the growing gay section of the District.

I agreed without hesitation.

:Take me forward, to the day it happened.:

Fuck you, I thought. You want me to relive the worst moment of my life and cheat me of one of the few good ones?

I remembered very little about what we talked about or where exactly we had coffee, or even what DuPont Circle looked like. What I remembered, with luxuriant detail, was the feel of her lips on mine when she kissed me good night. While I was growing up I'd come to understand that I wanted to be with women, but there had been no opportunity to put my feelings into practice. It wasn't until I went away to college that I had first held a woman, kissed her, touched her. Paranoia made most of the women unwilling for more than brief liaisons and guarded friendships. It wasn't that unexpected at a Bible college, but I'd been surprised to find it just the same at Princeton. Only a few would even say the word *lesbian* and the rest did not associate with those of us who did.

Laney was kissing me right out in the open, next to the Metro entrance. Her hands were under my jacket, and they warmed more than my skin. I was exhilarated by the freedom. Hopes and dreams that had nothing to do with career and law school blossomed. I was happier in that moment than I'd been in a long time and would ever be again.

I dodged the usual assortment of drug dealers and

prostitutes on my way home to my cheap-rent apartment. The dominoes were already falling, but I did not know that. I remembered that on Saturday I did my laundry and bought the few groceries I could afford. I missed the winter corn soup and dried tomatoes of home. I remembered that the weather on Sunday was glorious. The entire eastern seaboard was cold and clear, so I decided I would get out of the tiny apartment. What did the Patriots versus the Bears mean to me? The sky was high-country blue, and all of the museums on the Mall were free. The weather was so fine I walked to the farthest from the Metro and found myself in the Air and Space Museum.

I saw a notice that the shuttle launch had been postponed due to weather and that the IMAX theater would consequently not be broadcasting the liftoff today. That would have been exciting to see, I thought. Gigantic screen, rumbling sound. Now the shuttle simply had to lift off tomorrow or many political axes were going to fall on NASA's neck. I'd find out all about it at work. I'd also go out of my way to bump into Laney again.

I stood looking at Charles Lindbergh's plane, *The Spirit of St. Louis*, and marveled that anyone would have the audacity to cross an ocean in something so fragile. Was it courage or stupidity? I held the size of it in my mind far longer than I had actually stood there. I wanted to turn away, but something stopped me.

:It is an amazing thing. Let me look a moment.:

Fine, I thought. When it suits you, time just comes to a stop, but when I want to stop, no way.

The part of me not caught in my memories was deeply afraid. I knew the woman in my hogan was

32

doing this to me. I couldn't touch the fear — something had walled it away and I was trapped in her determined plan for reasons I couldn't begin to guess. I was completely at her mercy.

I wanted to ask why she was doing this to me. I formed words with my mind and directed them to where I heard the voice. *:Why? Why this?:*

I sensed surprise. *:It matters to me.:*

What a good reason, I thought. That certainly makes it okay to rummage through my past and put me through hell all over again. There was no response to my sarcasm.

We stared at the tiny airplane for a few moments longer, and my sense of amazement returned. The longer this went on, the more aware I was that she watched with me and shared my perceptions.

The size of the *Apollo 13* capsule shocked both of us — it was so small that I hardly believed three grown men would fit. It made me claustrophobic just to look inside.

:It sufficed.:

The onboard computer had no more memory than Atari video games. Yet people were willing to travel in outer space in a tin can, I thought. By comparison, the space shuttles seemed like luxury liners, but to me it was still a tin can with ten million little pieces to break or malfunction. At the time I didn't even know that only two shuttles were fully functional at any one time because so many parts were borrowed between the fleet of four crafts.

:Such courage.:

Courage? Believing something was safe just because it hadn't broken yet was foolhardy at best.

:Show me everything.:

I sensed eagerness now that we were so close. The presence with me in my memories wanted it all, so I gave it to her in all the tragic detail. I showed her the news accounts that confirmed the much-anticipated *Challenger* launch had indeed been postponed due to concerns about the weather. The predicted storms had not materialized, however, and the launch was scheduled for early Monday morning. They gave up the perfect launch window and warm weather. The probability of the O-rings disintegrating was vastly reduced in warm temperatures. I have often wondered how the person who had predicted the storm front felt about his or her mistake.

On Monday, in anticipation of the shuttle launch, the television in the conference room was tuned to CNN. By ten I had given up listening. There was a delay about a latch.

Tom kept calling NASA for updates beyond what the reporters covered. After the launch had been scrubbed for the day, he announced the story. Every word was there in my mind. "So Scobee sees that a bolt is broken on a latch and insists they fix it. What are they going to do? He's the commander. Besides, someone should have noticed it before the crew arrived. So some Lockheed know-nothing comes up to get the broken bolt out, but his power drill battery is dead. Someone goes to get another one but they're all dead, not one of them has enough charge to get the bolt out. The bolt is surrounded by fragile heat shields, so they can't just whack at it with a hammer. By the time they finally fix the thing, the cross-wind pattern on the Cape blows up and they had to give it up for the day."

Jerry was aghast. "They gave up yesterday's

perfect warm weather because some Air Force idiot decided a storm was coming in that stalled on the panhandle indefinitely. No networks tapping into the launch because everyone's up watching TV and ready for some good ol' American sports, and the news guys have got nothing else to do until kickoff. And they scratch today because of a dead drill battery? Bill is going to shit. They have to scrub the mission!"

Tom shook his head. "They're going to give it one last try tomorrow, and God help them if it doesn't go. They know the lost day will mean less time to refurbish the liftoff pad, but they think they have the crews to do it. Since the State of the Union is tomorrow night, I imagine that they're all getting an earful from the White House. NASA doesn't have a choice. They have to go tomorrow," Tom said. He noticed that I was listening. "Did that fax go on Friday?"

I nodded. "I've got the transmission receipt here somewhere."

He swelled up like a schoolyard bully. "Now they know the real score. At least the weather looks clear. Just cold — the citrus farmers are freaking. I'm going to have to do a progress report for Bill with copies to the entire oversight committee on this one. They're supposed to have redundant tool kits right at the launch pad, so two hundred people aren't waiting on a screwdriver. Christ."

I have often wondered if the man with the faulty drill ever considered what would have happened if he had made sure his battery had held a strong enough charge for the job.

"Why on earth did the congressman want to go up in one of those things?"

Tom looked at me as if I had lost my mind. The answer, to him at least, was obvious. "Senator Nelson sounds just great, doesn't it?"

Tuesday, January 28, 1986. This is it, I thought.
:I want to see it all.:
Yeah, yeah, I thought. *:Fine. You want my memories? You'll get them as I get to them.:*
"*Challenger* is a go," Tom announced. It was almost eleven-thirty. "I just heard from a buddy that the Air and Space Museum is going to show the NASA launch feed on their IMAX system. Anyone want to head down there?"

I had been thrilled. I knew it was the closest I would ever come to being there in person. Soon a group of seven or eight of us was hurrying down Independence Avenue toward the museum.

We took any seats available. The theater was mostly filled with what appeared to be school field trips. I settled in and picked up the launch control narrative. It was much more detailed than what was heard on TV. I had no idea what an orbiter aero-surface test was, but the closeups of the feed from NASA's cameras were spectacular on a projection screen two stories high.

"Look at the ice on everything," I said to Tom. Needles hung from every scaffold and walkway, making the shuttle look like a space-age winter post-card. "What happened to the warm weather?"

"Last night it dropped another twenty-five degrees. But freezing's not a problem. The sky is clear."

Engineers at Morton-Thiokol knew that freezing was a problem. Administrators at NASA hadn't been convinced.

I had quickly pieced together that the indicators at the bottom of the screen told who was speaking. Commander Scobee and Pilot Mike Smith were moving liquid oxygen feeders away from the shuttle at T minus 1:44. The drone of the time countdown came from a public affairs officer at Kennedy launch control in Florida.

It was the dispassionate voice that made me realize I was about to live it all again. I knew that begging to stop was useless. :*If you make me do this, you'll have to live with it too:*

:*I must know. This is an unprecedented opportunity.*:

I was horrified. Was this just an academic exercise? Forcing me into my past, making me live through this agony again, bringing the memories back so vividly — just to satisfy her own curiosity? Fuck you, I thought. I tried to stop the flow of memories, like hitting a pause button on a VCR. The pressure in my head became excruciating, then I couldn't hold it any more.

Judy Resnik's exuberant "All right" was barely audible as the theater sound system conveyed the booming rumble of the solid fuel boosters igniting. I clutched the arm of my chair in excitement and joined in the cheers and applause in the theater and from the observers in Florida. That angle did not show what other closeups would reveal: The primary and secondary O-rings on the right-hand rocket booster had failed; a burst of orange flame was visible on one side. Only the glassy aluminum oxides that resulted from the explosion held everything together.

They were already doomed.

Please let me stop — let me stop now! My memory self was cheering like at a sporting event, but my heartbeat had started the countdown. Ten seconds, twenty, thirty. At forty-nine seconds they encountered the most severe wind shear that any shuttle to date had experienced. The force of the shear shattered the glassy oxides, and the flame quickly traveled to the liquid hydrogen. Without the wind shear, the temporary seal might have held for another minute, when the only abort plan that would have saved their lives would have come into play.

The shuttle was a dot with a gigantic plume of exhaust behind it. The voice-over had switched to a public affairs officer in Houston as the Johnson Space Center took over monitoring. Commander Scobee said he was throttling up. T plus 1:10.

I willed history to change. Anything to hold the breach together — one more minute, just fifty more seconds, forty-nine, forty-eight. *Please . . . God, please.*

There was another brilliant flare of orange flame, then puffs of black smoke. The exhaust plume divided in two like a forked tongue while the central orbiter was shaken into pieces. The external tank to which the orbiter was connected blossomed into a fireball. The shuttle itself was hidden in the billows of smoke. The wings were torn off, the shuttle bay vibrated loose, and the still intact crew cabin began to fall. Pilot Mike Smith said, "Uh-oh."

Houston went silent, as did the theater. On screen the solid rocket boosters were spiraling out of control. Two brilliant flashes made me gasp — then the sky was filled with rocket debris. A lone parachute appeared and drifted slowly toward the sea.

When the voice from Houston came back, it was tense. I heard the words *major malfunction* but could not drag my gaze from the screen. The sky was empty except for feathers of white smoke trails. I had just sat there, completely unable to comprehend what my eyes had witnessed.

:Thank you.:

:You bitch, you heartless bitch.: I could feel tears running down my cheeks, into my ears. *:We're not stopping now!:*

The other staffers were leaving, but I just sat there. Kids were crying, their teachers were crying. The projection switched to news commentators who reported that the parachute belonged to one of the exploded boosters, not to a member of the crew. A so-called expert explained how the shuttle was designed to land after an aborted flight, and the various escape options the astronauts had. The expert did not mention that those plans only came into play at T plus 2 minutes.

NASA announced "that the vehicle had impacted into the water" and that a recovery effort was being coordinated.

I managed to stir myself when it was clear there was no more news at that time. The guards at the House Office Building were ashen and grave as they discussed whether anyone could still be alive. A commentator on the television behind them was speculating that the parachute was the crew's escape plan. I already knew that was false.

:I have seen all this in other ways.:

Tough, I thought. *:You don't know it the way I do. It's all there in those references in my bookcase. They had no escape plan during the most dangerous part of* *the mission. It cost too much and added too much weight to be able to save their lives during the first two minutes. You wanted to know — then know everything, including my despair.:*

Hours flowed by. Nelson arrived back from his canceled engagements, and every television in the office was tuned to a different news agency. The sun was going down when all the stations began a press conference from Kennedy. Nelson paced angrily in front of the television in his office, muttering, "They're all dead, why don't they just say so?" He knew that better than anybody. I wondered then, and I still wonder, if anyone had told the civilians on the flight — McAuliffe and Jarvis — that if anything went wrong in the first two minutes, there was no saving them.

The solemn-faced representative from NASA didn't say they were dead. He said there was no evidence any of them had survived. To the many technical questions he replied that he did not know. Then someone asked about the weather. The representative said that everything was in good shape for a launch.

Still, nothing was said about the astronauts. Had their bodies been found? Had the shuttle itself been recovered? Had their families been told? My God, I thought, they were probably all standing there at the Cape, watching it happen. Wasn't McAuliffe's class from New Hampshire there as well? All those kids watching their parents and their teacher die, and not knowing how or why. Parents were watching their children die. I knew I would never get over it, so how could the families?

Reporters asked about the pressure that had been put on NASA to get mission 51-L in the air to clear the pad for the next mission. They weren't crass enough to mention the State of the Union — that finger-pointing would come later. What about a high-level meeting called by one of the contractors yesterday? Had it been Rockwell? Was Rockwell concerned about the ice hitting the heat shields? If it wasn't Rockwell, then who? What had been the problem? Had *Challenger* really been ready to fly?

Nelson stopped pacing. The answer was unequivocal. "There was absolutely no pressure to get this particular launch off . . ."

I felt dizzy. I sat down at my desk and dug around until I found the fax I had sent on Friday. The final paragraph, that I had suggested and written, imprinted itself forever on my mind: *I'm sure that by the time we meet at Appropriations the question of Challenger 51-L will be moot, and that important issues of space station funding will not get tabled to make room for discussion of launch priorities.*

I was cold all over and wouldn't ever feel truly warm again.

All that was left to show her were the investigation reports, all the journalism, and the certain knowledge that political pressure to get the flight in the air had led NASA officials to ignore safety warnings. They had been warned about both the damage that falling ice would do to the heat shields, and then the disintegration of the O-rings in freezing temperatures. The day before the launch, engineers from Rockwell had expressed concern that ice would damage the heat shields. Later reviews of the tape would show the ice doing exactly that. Whether the damage would have endangered the crew during reentry was, of course, impossible to know.

That same day, engineers from Morton-Thiokol faxed thirteen pages of evidence that the O-rings would break down if launched at the predicted launch temperature, which was thirty degrees colder than any previous launch or test. They had strongly urged a no-launch, the first time they had done so in twelve years. NASA had asked them to reconsider. Managers and engineers at Thiokol argued well into the night, then the managers reported that the evidence was inconclusive and gave NASA a go-ahead.

The investigators would comment that the engineering data had been stupefyingly detailed. Nowhere had the engineers summarized in plain language the basis for their no-launch recommendation: the thirty-eight-foot-diameter O-rings *always* showed erosion in launch temperatures on real and test launches below sixty-six degrees. They had no data for a launch where the O-rings would be at twenty-two degrees, but their data extrapolated to a complete breakdown of both primary and secondary O-rings. Nowhere did they state the almost certain possibility of a disastrous explosion.

:Busy people sometimes do not understand facts.:

It was no excuse, I raged. People with power had ignored warnings. Where was NASA's long-lauded reputation for doing whatever it took, whatever the cost, to keep their people safe? What had made otherwise rational, scientific people turn their back on even a hint that launch conditions were abnormal enough to evaluate the stability of the entire system at freezing temperatures?

The day it happened I knew that political pressure to get the launch off had made them deaf to any voice of caution. NASA had provided text for the President's speech, but officials would later claim they had felt no pressure at all, that they hadn't been correctly informed about the risks. I can't even begin to imagine the helplessness the engineers themselves had felt that morning when they'd seen the temperature for real, when they'd watched the launch and hoped against hope that they were wrong. But I knew how I felt.

I had been a part of the political pressure. I had helped fan the flame. I had threatened taking away money from other projects unless the launch happened. Money was already so tight at NASA that they cannibalized spare parts for the shuttles from each other. Any threat to hold up any funds had to be taken seriously.

I had helped kill them.

One last thing, I thought. I showed her the memorial service and the faces of the families. I imagined myself trying to say how sorry I was, but they stared silently at me with accusing eyes.

I could suddenly feel the cold floor under me, and I rolled to my side, as wretched with tears and grief as I had been thirteen years ago.

Bitterly, I asked, "Was that what you wanted? Did you see what you wanted to see?"

The voice didn't answer, but I knew, somehow, that not all the tears washing through my mind were my own.

:Sleep. Forget.:

3

I floated up from sleep with a tranquillity I hadn't known for years. I deeply inhaled cold air, then pressed my fingers to my lips. My warm breath caressed my fingers — a sensation so alive that I did it again and smiled.

I was on the floor, wrapped in a blanket. I didn't remember falling asleep there, but it hardly mattered. I felt wonderfully rested. When I got to my feet and went into the bathroom, however, I caught sight of myself in the tiny mirror over the sink. My slovenly reflection sent a shock through my body. Bemused, I touched my tangled hair, cracked lips, overgrown eyebrows. Lines grooved around my mouth like brands. I looked down at my body — I was too thin, almost gaunt. I caught sight of old and new scars on my hands. Several of my fingernails were recently torn, and the rest were bitten to the quick. I had expected to see someone much younger in the mirror, with curls of red hair and bright green eyes. Instead I saw my grandmother, but without any of the light that had always been a part of her.

I felt as if I were waking from a long sleep to find myself old and wasted. What had happened to me? I just could not remember. I scrubbed my face and then dug through the disorderly medicine cabinet until I found the long-forgotten eyebrow tweezers. A few minutes later the skin around my eyebrows was red from my relentless attack, but I no longer looked like a troglodyte.

I stared into the hollow eyes in the mirror and swallowed hard. Why was I living in a hogan? Where exactly was I? Then the floodgates of memory opened — the explosion, the crew cabin falling, the fax I had written and sent. My hollow eyes were just a reflection of the emptiness I had felt inside me for thirteen years. How could I even have forgotten it for one moment?

Something scuffled behind me.

I spun on my heel. A woman was watching me — that woman, the one who . . . the one who . . .

"Don't be afraid," the woman said.

I lunged to the kitchen cupboard and ripped open the drawer. I clutched my biggest carving knife as I backed as far away as I could from . . . from an impossibility.

"You have nothing to fear from me." The woman did not seem perturbed by the knife.

"Who the hell are you?" I tingled all over . . . I was going to faint again. I waved the knife with one hand and scrabbled at the wall with the other as if I could hold reality together with my fingertips. She could not be Christa McAuliffe. "You aren't Betsy or Lisa because they don't look that much like their sister." I pushed away from the wall. "And you're too old to be their daughters, or her daughter Caroline."

The woman blinked, as if listening to inner voices telling her what lie to fob off on me.

I took a shaky step forward, knife raised. "I want the truth. Who are you? Why are you doing this to me?"

"I never intended to do anything to you," the woman said earnestly. She cleared her hoarse throat. "I just want to know where I am."

I was shaking my head. "Try again. Because I don't believe you."

The woman looked at me intently for a long moment. I had a peculiar sensation of vertigo.

:I don't remind you of anyone. You can trust me.:

She broke into a toothy grin. "Are you making something to eat?"

I had forgotten why I was holding the knife. I set it down quickly. "I can open a couple of cans of stew. You're probably starved."

"I am. The coffee is hot, but it's not —"

"Filling, don't I know that? I might even have some frozen biscuits." I turned to the kitchenette, then paused. "You know, I don't even know your name."

"Call me Sharon, please."

A tight confusion buzzed in my brain. For a moment, I thought I recognized the woman. "Do I know you from somewhere?"

:I don't remind you of anyone. You can trust me.:

Sharon blinked. "I don't know your name either."

"Amanda Martin." The confusion in my head melted away with a momentary throb. I felt much better. Giddy, even.

"It's a pleasure to meet you. And thank you for your hospitality."

I found the biscuits and put them in the oven. "My hospitality isn't much. This is quite a ways from civilization."

"Where exactly? I am really curious as to just how lost I am." Sharon looked so helpless that I wondered how she managed on her own. Typical tourist. I braced myself for what would seem like an eternity until she left.

As we ate our simple meal, I formulated firmer, and slightly higher, opinions about her. Sharon seemed like a slightly clueless yet bright and amiable person. I could not let her walk out to Chinle by herself — she was coyote fodder on her own. Besides, I was starting to not mind so much her being there. I realized that I had been lonely, but had accepted the loneliness as part of my penance.

She was looking at the map with a slightly bemused expression. "You're absolutely sure we're here." She pointed at the northeast corner of Arizona close to the New Mexico border.

"If we walk east about a mile, we're in New Mexico," I said. "Not that the canyons care."

"Boundaries matter little to nature." She furrowed her brow, then drew a line across Arizona to Los Angeles. Then she laughed. "I guess I should never trust pilots. I was told we were here." She pointed to the vicinity of Barstow, California, halfway between Los Angeles and Las Vegas.

"Then you need to sue somebody. Was it a charter?"

For some reason, she found my question very amusing. She laughed as if she hadn't had much experience at it, which was confusing since everything about her suggested vitality and humor. "A charter is one way to put it. I'm going to Los Angeles to meet friends of friends, and then I'm going home." She gestured toward her all-weather suit. "I have gifts and messages."

I carried the dishes to the sink and realized I was still wearing my robe. While I changed into some sweats of my own, I took in the significance of the utter quiet beyond the windows — no wind, no thrum of rain, no spatter of sandy gravel against the walls, none of the usual night noises.

Snow, I thought, winter's last gasp. "You may not get far very soon," I said with a sinking heart. She'd upset my equilibrium enough. I could already tell it would be hard to be alone again. "The roads are going to be unplowed for probably two days. I have a Jeep about an hour's walk from here, but that's in good weather, and there's no guarantee the car will start in this weather. It wouldn't be pretty for us if it didn't. There's nobody else living in the canyon during the winter. Just me. Hell, there's no guarantee the Jeep will even be there." I parked much closer during summer. When I parked that far out, it wasn't that uncommon for someone to "borrow" it with every intention of bringing it back before I missed it.

With more ease than I would have dreamed possible, I said, "You'll just have to put up with me for a few days — the weather is due to turn warm soon." All my years in the canyon told me that.

"I'm sure I can manage the walk if I start early tomorrow."

I seriously doubted it. She didn't recognize the difference between six-thousand-foot-plus canyon country and sea-level desert. Left alone with a can opener and a crate of canned goods, she'd probably starve to death.

I opened the hogan door. It was snowing all right. Six inches so far.

She came up behind me and peered out. It was completely dark beyond the light from the doorway. White flakes floated into the light, looking harmless. "Oh, I see." She stepped around me and let some of the downy flakes settle on her hand. Like a child she popped a flake-covered fingertip into her mouth. In the feeble light it almost looked like she was glowing.

Abruptly, she turned and ran into the darkness.

"Hey! It's freezing out there." I sounded like a worried mom, but she had no coat and only socks on her feet.

"I'm okay," she called back. She panted into view,

covered with snow and looking thoroughly exhilarated. Something stirred in me, a feeling I hadn't recognized in too many years.

I told myself it was just the effect of spending too much time alone.

She tromped inside and stomped snow off her socks. "That was great. I'll have no trouble walking out to the town. Twelve miles? I'll be okay."

I seriously doubted it. I started to close the door but she stopped me, cocking her head to one side.

I put my hands behind my back to keep them from doing anything untoward. "What's wrong?"

"Nothing," she said. "It's just so quiet. Reminds me of home."

Her animated, attractive face was just a few inches from mine. "Where's home?"

"A long way away." She lifted her gaze from the falling snow and looked at me curiously. Then her expression changed — I knew that look. It was how Laney had looked at me. How I had undoubtedly looked at Laney. Then Sharon drew back sharply and said lightly, "I was raised in a very quiet environment. I knew I was loved, but there were no words."

I closed the door and stepped away as quickly as I could without being in full retreat. I thought of the endless pandemonium of the Christian school my grandmother had run and felt unwillingly sorry for her. "I don't think I would have liked that."

"I didn't know any difference." She stretched her arms as if she was just enjoying the feel of it. "It was like a hospital."

"Now I know I wouldn't have liked that. More coffee?"

"No, thank you."

I didn't blame her. I glanced at the clock — it was nearly midnight. Where had the evening gone? "You must be tired." I wasn't, but I certainly ought to have been.

"Actually, I am. Very." She was smiling again, as if being tired was just another welcome experience.

I sized up my narrow bed. Two was right out, unless the two concerned really did not care how close they were to each other.

"I can sleep in the chair, really," she said.

"Are you sure?" There was something pampered about her, as if she had just gotten out of a nunnery. No, *pampered* was the wrong word. *Unworldly. Inexperienced.* "Have you ever done that before?"

"Honestly?" She turned her clear brown eyes on me. I was momentarily dizzy, then the feeling faded. "No, I haven't. But I'm longing to give it a try."

I grinned in spite of myself. She had to be in her late thirties, and yet she reminded me of an eleven-year-old on her first camping trip. "Then you can be my guest," I said. I set the room heater to come on periodically, gave her the best and warmest blankets, then settled down on my bed.

I surprised myself by falling asleep. I was surprised that I knew I was asleep and that my sleep dropped me into my past.

I had still been in shock when I'd left work that terrible day. I hadn't even seen Laney in the elevator.

"Are you just going to ignore me?" Her voice cut into my thoughts as I reached the building entrance. Fortunately for me, she seemed unperturbed.

"I'm a little — I just can't stop thinking about it."

She knew what "it" was. "Neither can I. What do you think happened?"

"I don't know." I wouldn't know for weeks. Some of the information would be months in being released to public scrutiny. "But I did something . . ."

We were out on the street now. The temperature was dropping by the second. Laney stopped walking when my voice trailed off. "What's wrong?"

"I . . . it was my fault!" The words burst out of me.

"That's nonsense," she said. "It couldn't possibly be."

My words tumbled over themselves. I knew I was not making sense. "The press conference said that one of the contractors was worried about the flight and they lied — they said there was no pressure to get it in the air and there was, I know there was, because I wrote it, and I faxed it." I started to cry.

"Let's go talk," Laney said.

We talked at a coffee bar, we talked on the Metro. We talked on the way to her apartment. My mind sped through the details of what we said. I was hurrying toward the one decent memory — there it was.

Her hands were on my skin, and it felt glorious. For a moment, just a moment, I forgot about seven dead astronauts. I surged against her thigh, and we strained against each other's need. Her heartbeat sounded in my ears. I could feel it with my fingertips on her ribs, with them deep inside her. Her mouth was like a flame on my body, burning away time. Our tight, furious motion stopped in a gasp of delight.

"Wow," she said.

"That felt fabulous." I inhaled the perfume on my fingertips. She caught me at it and reached for me with hunger, but I was already remembering the dead, and this time passion would not let me forget.

I tried. She tried. For several months we both tried to pretend I was okay. I was falling apart, one day at a time. I got "laid off," and Laney was getting both weary and wary of my histrionics. I would sob uncontrollably, then go on eating binges or all-day walks when I forgot to eat or drink.

The night I reached for her and she actually shrank from my touch, I knew I had to go home. Home for me would always be the other world of the reservation. It promised me escape and silence.

I was asleep, or so I thought, and I could feel the sweet pressure of Laney's forgiving good-bye kiss. I'd lied when I said I would stay in touch. She said when I worked things out she would love to hear from me. She said I was too hard on myself, but stopped there so we wouldn't fight again. We hadn't even had the chance to find out if we could love each other.

I relived Laney's passion once more, then once more. It felt so real, as if I was in her arms again.

:I'm sorry — I didn't know you had lost so much.:

I was so lonely. So very lonely. I missed women. I missed people. But I still hadn't fixed it.

I slowly became aware that I wasn't alone in my sleep. I was aware that Sharon was sleeping too. Her thoughts meandered into mine, bright with curiosity but without overt purpose. *:Laney?:*

I happily showed her my memories of Laney, then her brightness gave them full light. The curve of Laney's hip, the smooth texture of her skin, the way her thigh felt against my cheek. I shuddered at the way Laney kissed the freckles that were dusted across my arms, shoulders and breasts. We had been hungry for each other all the time, as if feasting led to starvation, as if we knew we would never get enough.

:The curve of her hip . . .:

I traced it with my fingertip. Here it was warm to the touch, here a little cooler. The silky hair between her legs tickled my fingertip. Silk here, salty-sweetness there. I felt it on my lips and chin, tasted it on my tongue. She gasped, and the gasp was echoed through my mind and back again, louder.

:Don't stop . . .:

I leaned over Laney's body and breathed in the sexual sweat and perfume. She was beautiful in her need. She was the only person who ever called me Amy. "Amy, please don't tease."

:Don't tease . . .:

She surrounded my fingers with yielding strength. She cried out, "Amy, please, Amy please."

:Amy . . .:

:Sharon?:

The new voice was not my thoughts. I tried to gather my wits, all the while knowing I was fast asleep.

:Sela? What . . .:

The confusion Sharon felt pushed me away from her. Our minds separated with a rough sensation of tearing. I felt bereft of something I'd never known.

Then the buzzing of voices, like angry bees, came back. They were arguing again.

4

When I was very young, I think five or so, my grandmother took me on a train trip to visit relatives. They argued the whole time, about me mostly. I remember sitting outside and hearing the rise and fall of their bitter voices and wishing I was anywhere else but there. My father had died in Vietnam when I was minus three months old. When I was two, my mother died because she waited too long to go to the hospital for treatment of pneumonia. I was sent to my grand-parents, who were in the process of moving to a new mission, one where there would be lots of kids. What could be a better environment than a Christian church and school?

As the train clanked on our return trip from Salt Lake City to Kingman, Arizona, I had kept quiet. My grandmother was angrier than I had ever seen her — not that she took it out on me. But I was miserable to see the brilliant red spots in her cheeks and the way she was twisting her handkerchief. I hated it when people argued.

"If you raise her with savages she'll become one." I'd heard one aunt say that very loudly. When all was said and done, I don't think a single one of them offered me any other kind of life. However, they'd still vehemently told my grandmother that she was making a mess of me, all because I'd never seen a Barbie doll or television and when I played cowboys and Indians I was happy to play the Indian but then I played to win. I'd been on my best behavior, I'd really tried, but nothing I did made me fit in with my cousins.

It was a curious place to live, between two worlds. The Navajo kids were nice enough to me. I had best friends and bitter enemies, but a barrier remained that I could not cross because I was not Navajo and never would be. When the other kids started dating, none of the Navajo boys asked me. And the few other white kids were too wild for my grandparents. I suppose that would have hurt more than it did if I hadn't suspected by then that the last thing I wanted was a boy asking me out.

I was eighteen before I again left the reservation, this time for Bible college, courtesy of my grandfather's ties. The genuine interest of the college president had put me on the path to Princeton's law school with a partial scholarship.

Those years had been exhausting—I had worked every job I could find to fill the financial gaps. I had lived on peanuts and rice sometimes for days. I had not been too proud to ask for the half-rotten fruits and vegetables the produce market was going to throw away. I had been desperately homesick and had missed my grandparents. It still pained me that they'd both died while I was too far away to get home in time to say good-bye.

My Princeton years were my Long Walk. I wasn't Navajo, but the stories Hosteen Sam had taught me were still my primers for survival. In between prayers for deliverance of my soul I'd think about one of Hosteen Sam's Blessing Way songs. I had learned to hear the nuances of wind and the rustle of rabbit claws and the hesitation in a person's speech that speaks more volumes than their words ever could. There was no telling what I might have made of my life if I hadn't pressed Start on that fax transmission. I thought it made me so smart, knowing the game of political manipulation. I'd forgotten about people's lives, as if that was a good thing. Seven people had paid the price.

I was asleep and yet I was sifting through my thoughts as if wide awake. The past had all come back to me for some reason. I was in the past because . . . I strained, but I could not remember why.

The clicking of the room heater brought me a little further out of my sleep. My body was heavy with fulfillment — a sensation I hadn't known for so many years. I wanted to stay inside the feeling, languish in it, but the buzzing of a distant conversation was waking me up. I was remembering . . . it was so hard. I'd done so much remembering and forgetting in the last twelve hours. The way my brain was spinning wasn't right.

The conversation came closer, then with a snap of awareness, I could hear it clearly again. Like my long-ago relatives, they argued with a presumption of familiarity and the freedom to say anything no matter how hurtful because it was between family. The bitterness was tangible.

:It was not your decision, and not for you to take.: This voice was harsh and cutting, like a flash of steel.

:If I had ever had any idea what you were keeping me from, I would have insisted on coming sooner.: That was Sharon, I knew the vibrations of her thoughts. I could still feel the resonance in places that I had long ignored. :I can't go anywhere but here, you made sure of that, Sela:

Sela was cold and withdrawn. :It was our only option, you know that.:

:I've lost too much time already. Snow — snow, you can't imagine what it's really like. Experiences do not compare to books or images on a screen.:

:You're losing your perspective. I knew this would happen.: Sela was obviously from the I'm-always-right school of thought. :You had no right to do that with her.:

:Maybe not . . . and I don't know if I can stop myself from doing it again.:

:You are coming back the moment it can be arranged.:

:No. Not until I'm ready. If this is all there will ever be, then I will drink the cup to the very bottom.:

Sharon's conviction was heartfelt and implacable. Sela kept arguing, but I found myself rooting for Sharon. I wanted her to stay, to lift me up from the depths. I wanted her arms around me — or were they Laney's arms? I was forgetting again, or remembering again.

I was so confused. Where was Laney? Who was Sharon? Sharon, who looked like Christa McAuliffe, who had sat at my table and eaten my food, tangled in my past and my dreams and all the while . . .

. . . all the while . . .

It was difficult to fix on a single thought, but with concentration I could picture myself earlier in the evening, going through the motions of hospitality, giving information without asking questions, and simply not recognizing that I had watched the woman who was dining with me die thirteen years ago.

I wanted to wake up now and get my knife back — what had made me surrender it in the first place? Who was she? What kind of power did she have over me?

I struggled to consciousness because I knew my life depended on it. Certainly my sanity did. She had already done something to me that could not be forgiven. She had made me relive it all, and the grief that boiled in me was as fresh as the day it happened. I'd spent thirteen years trying to learn to bear it, and she had brought it all back to satisfy some sort of academic curiosity.

As if that wasn't enough, she had let her mind wander into my dreams and fantasies. My body was heavy with satisfaction and already swelling with desire for more, without even a touch. She had made me want more of her, and that was wrong too. Well, at least my head thought it was wrong. My body was having second thoughts.

For now, my head was winning. If I ever wanted to

get myself back to where I had stubbornly climbed these past thirteen years, she had to undo what she had done. She had to help me start over. I managed to get one leg off the bed.

Sela was angry. :*You should have left well enough alone.*:

:*How could I when she had been there, seen it all happen? It gave me a perspective I could only guess at before. See it from her eyes, Sela. We never guessed at the depth of anguish even strangers felt — see it from her eyes.*:

:*I don't want to. I don't need to. You've lost all distance. I knew you weren't ready!*:

:*Ready for what? Another year of nothingness? Of intimacy without sensation? A lifetime without purpose, an eternity without the sun on my face?*:

My balance wasn't great, so I took slow, deliberate steps. A slight lightening at the windows and door announced the first light of morning. She had abandoned the chair and was wrapped in the blankets on the rug, utterly still, too distracted to hear me. Maybe she was a telepath. I don't know if I believe in that. But I could hear what she was thinking, and God knows she seemed to pry through my mind with impunity. I heard the voice of another. Sharon called her Sela. I was not going mad. Or maybe I was. Sanity hadn't been my strong point since it happened.

It didn't matter who Sharon was. All that mattered was that she leave me alone. I decided that she didn't exist. I was wrestling with Snake or Coyote People. They wanted to make me crazy, steal my language and my sight.

I am not crazy, I thought. :*I will not let you drive me over the edge.*: I'd been dangling myself over cliffs for thirteen years. If I decided to fall, it would be my doing, not some demon's doing.

My head cleared suddenly, and I realized I had my hands around her throat. She was choking for air, her arms flailing weakly at me. I was awake and she was real. I snatched my hands back as if she were on fire, then stumbled out of her reach.

She choked and coughed for several minutes, then calmed somewhat with raspy breathing.

"Tell me the truth."

She coughed one last time and sat up. Her voice was even more hoarse. "You think you'll get the truth by killing me?"

"It got you out of my head, and I'll do it for sure if you don't stay out."

She had the ability to look embarrassed and pained, but I wasn't convinced. "I'm sorry. I really am. I didn't have any right to do it."

I realized I didn't know what "it" meant. Did she mean making me relive the tragedy of the *Challenger*? Or did she mean the undeniable sharing when I had dreamed about Laney — if it even was a dream. It had been too real and too satisfying to be a dream. I suddenly didn't want to ask. "Sorry because I knew what you were doing, or sorry because you did it?"

"Both."

"And if I'd never found out? Would you be sorry?"

"Yes," she said firmly. "I'm sorry that it hurt you. I knew that it was going to, but I thought I could make you forget when it was over. But you forgot everything instead of just me in your mind — I've never worked with anyone like you before."

It was getting lighter as the sun reflected off of last night's snow. I could see her earnest expression, but I would not be beguiled by her again. "Are you trying to tell me you're a piss-poor telepath? I don't even believe in telepaths!"

A smile flashed across her face, making her cheeks go all chipmunky. How could she be so harmless in appearance, so appealing on the surface? I'm thinking she's Christa, I thought. She wasn't. Everything I'd read about Christa McAuliffe, which was a lot, suggested she would have never been cruel to anyone for any reason. Christa McAuliffe would have no idea how to slide into someone's mind and make them feel as if every inch of their body had been consumed by ecstasy.

"I know you don't believe. Of course you don't. I've gone about this all wrong. I've botched it from the very beginning." :*I know you don't believe me, but I can be in your mind.*:

"Stop that!" I jumped to my feet and raised my fists. "Stop it!" I took two steps toward her, then found I couldn't move.

"I'm sorry," she said. "I just want you to believe what I am because if you don't, you'll start thinking you're crazy. I don't want that on my conscience."

I could move again. I stared at her, furious. "That is so uncalled for!"

"How many times do I have to say I'm sorry?" She rested her head on one knee. "I have the worst headache."

"Maybe it'll hurt less if you stop messing around with my head."

"Probably." She looked up at me. "But you believe me now, don't you?"

"No," I said stubbornly. I absolutely, totally, completely for ever and ever did not believe her. I didn't believe her so much that I knew I was lying to myself, which is something I rarely do.

This was so unfair. Did I really deserve this? After all the years of self-imposed penance, of loneliness and flirting with death and madness, did I really deserve this?

"You do believe me," she said. "That's enough. My being here is a mistake," she added. "I had no idea that you specifically existed, or that even someone like you existed."

"What is someone like me?" My fury was still there, but my traitor body, watching the way her hands moved when she talked, the way she wrinkled her nose — my traitor body was telling me to move closer.

She waved one hand at our surroundings. "To begin with, I wasn't aware that any Americans lived like this. No home office, no minivan, no swimming pool."

"You watch too much mainstream television."

This amused her, and it irritated me that she was smiling again. Was she ever serious? "That is undoubtedly true. All I know of you is from what can be picked up by a satellite dish."

"Okay," I said slowly. "You're some sort of spy." I had a vision of Alec Guinness playing a cold war agent of espionage. Sharon was a long way from that image.

"Some sort of, yes. Not that kind."

I glowered at her.

"Sorry," she said weakly. "It was too vivid to ignore.

"And being a some-sort-of-spy is not the whole truth."

"You're right, it's not." She examined her fingers.

"So what do we do now?"

"You help me on my way, and that's it."

"I can't do that." I didn't want her to go. My body was making that abundantly clear.

"Why not? I assure you I have no ill intentions toward you or anybody for that matter."

I couldn't afford to believe her, for reasons that had nothing to do with my more primitive urges. "If that was true, you wouldn't look like that."

"I look how I look. This is how I was born."

"You're a dead ringer for a dead woman."

"I know." The air felt thick with unspoken truth.

Did she ever think about anyone but herself? "Just seeing you made me faint. Can you imagine what would happen if her kids saw you or her husband? Have you any idea of the pain you could cause?"

She blinked. "No, I hadn't thought of that." There was a hint of tears in her eyes. Crocodile tears, I thought. "We never thought anyone in this part of the world would recognize me. There seemed so little chance of anyone anywhere thinking that I look like my moth —" She bit back the word, but it was too late.

I stared at her, full of disdain. "You're full of shit. She can't be your mother. She had two children, and they're half your age."

She didn't answer, only looked at me. I felt the buzzing of her thoughts and the voice that she had been arguing with.

"Stop it!"

The buzzing stopped.

Her gaze narrowed, and her bright curiosity was in

full evidence. "You're really not supposed to be aware of it. I wonder why you are? Is it because we're so alone out here, or do you have some sort of special skill?"

"I'm not going to be your science project. You can go get your research someplace else. In fact, you can go fuck yourself." My thoughts, my life — none of it was her business.

"You're right, it's not my business," she said.

Flabbergasted, I spluttered out, "That is so incredibly rude!"

Her lips tightened. "I'm not so much reading as trying to dodge the thoughts you're broadcasting all over the place. It's impossible *not* to read your mind."

"Oh! So this is all *my* fault! Don't you people have some sort of code? Some sort of rules about invading other people's privacy?"

"Now *you've* been watching too much television."

I couldn't believe I was even talking about the subject with this, this stranger, who was walking around with a dead woman's body.

She frowned. "My body is my own."

"Stop that!" I shook with anger. "Just stop it!"

She put her hands over her eyes. "Do you think you could get a handle on your emotions? I'm willing to try, but you're making it hard."

I took several deep breaths, not knowing what to believe or do next.

She finally looked up. "I've tried to make you blank. I don't have very much practice at it. It's the only way I've ever communicated. I really don't mean to hurt you more than I already have."

That reminded me. "So why was making me show you the explosion so important?"

She pursed her lips and ran one hand through her hair. "Considering how I look, what do you think the answer is?"

"Are you going to try to claim she's your mother again? I know too much to believe you."

"I'm not supposed to tell you the truth. I'm not supposed to tell anyone the truth. I'm supposed to deliver my messages, get used to ... here ... and go home. That's all." She did not sound very happy about it.

I was getting such conflicting signals. Her behavior was sometimes ruthless and cunning, but right now she was like a confused kid. My impression that she had led a cloistered life was even stronger. I was no longer afraid of her, but perhaps I should have been.

My body, which had no semblance of impartiality, sat down on the blankets beside her. "Don't you think you owe me an explanation? It's going to take me a long time to get back to where I was." The explosion flashed in my mind, as richly detailed as if it had only been yesterday.

The tears in her eyes were genuine. "I'm not perfect. I don't know what to do. What I did wasn't right, but making even more mistakes won't fix it."

"Well, I'll tell you this. I can't think of an explanation, not for the way you look, not for what you seem to be. So I think anything you told me I probably wouldn't believe."

She did not seem comforted by that. I could sense how conflicted she was, as if our brief communication by mind had made me more sensitive to her.

Slowly, she said, "She isn't my mother, but I'm her daughter."

I said dryly, "Well, that helps."

She looked away. "Between the time of the explosion and the time she died — how long was it?"

The question pained me. "No one knows. At most, two minutes and forty-five seconds. They're certain that Judy Resnik was definitely alive. It's likely they were all alive."

"It was long enough to make decisions? Hard decisions?"

"Someone decided to explode the rocket boosters after they broke off so they wouldn't come down in a populated area. Judy Resnik activated her oxygen, and she probably activated oxygen for others."

"But there was time enough to make a decision."

I nodded, having no idea what she was getting at.

She took a deep breath, as if getting ready for a jump off a high dive. "They were alive as they fell. Nothing could save them. They died when they hit the water."

Images of the crew cabin falling at more than two hundred miles per hour overwhelmed me. At that speed, the ocean was like cement. I whispered, "How do you know they were alive?"

"We were watching too."

"But you said — you told that other person you hadn't seen it before."

She was direct and serious. "Not from your perspective. You were looking up." She swallowed hard. "Everything I have ever been shown or told about it was from those who were looking down."

I stared at her for the longest time, trying to

process what she was saying. Then I laughed. It was ludicrous. "You delivered that really well. I have to hand it to you. You might even believe it yourself."

She stared at me until I stopped laughing. It took a few minutes.

"It was long enough for someone to make a hard decision and to do something recklessly dangerous. Sela — the person you hear me talking to — was the one who made that decision. I would not be here if she hadn't taken an enormous chance. Because of her, I am a living being, a human being, and I'm here just to look around."

"And I am Marie of Romania." She stared at me blankly. "What, they don't have Dorothy Parker on satellite?"

"Think about it," she urged. "What else explains what you see and what you've experienced?"

"Hallucinations. Insanity. A migraine. I'll believe all of that before I believe in little green men. Or women."

She seized my hand, startling me. "I'm flesh, just like you. I am human. You are the first human I've ever had contact with after a lifetime of waiting."

I shook off her grasp. "That's nonsense. I'm willing to believe you might have some extra mental abilities, and I'm willing to believe that you have some mysterious purpose for coming here to torment me. Maybe it's to perfect your impersonation of her —"

"I am not claiming to be her —"

"Maybe you figure if you can fool me, you can fool everybody. Claim you were rescued by little green men and now they've sent you back to earth. You'd be on the talk show circuit in no time."

My suppositions were making her angry, and I was

glad. "I am not her! I am myself. You have no idea what being human costs me, you have no idea of the worlds closed to me because my DNA comes from this backwater planet —"

Her charade was getting too funny. "Backwater? Backwater to what? Some fabulous Planet of Rescued Astronauts in the center of the hippest part of the galaxy?"

She was good and mad. I could feel it in my head. "This planet is so far fucking away from everything we have to sleep half the way here —"

"You're learning all the human traits — swearing, wanting to live in the fashionable zip code —"

Her disdain would have been searing if what she said wasn't so ridiculous. "Not even the vegans want your zip code, and that's as close as it gets."

I whistled. "You're delusional. If you grew up in outer space, where'd you learn English? How come you know idiomatic speech? How do you even know what a zip code is?" I had her.

Her lip curled as if my intelligence was in question. "Your entire culture is bouncing around off of satellite dishes a child could intercept. I've seen your sporting contests, your television programs, listened to your radio." She changed her language, and I didn't understand a word. "There, I just said you're an idiot in Spanish, Russian, French, Dutch, Mandarin and Japanese. All of what you are is up there, and I have spent my entire life learning all of it. It's all I have ever had as experiences. You are the first person I've actually spoken aloud to."

Oh, man. I got up, chuckling. "And I thought I was two kernels short of a bushel. How do you expect anyone to believe you?"

She was gritting her teeth. "I don't. You asked for the truth; I gave it to you. All you have to do now is show me the way to the road."

The buzzing started again. The other voice was back.

Her response was unequivocal, and I heard it loud and clear. *:Sela, shut the fuck up!:*

"Okay," I said. "You speak American pretty darned well. I guess that's from all the cable television you get in space." All the while I brushed my teeth and washed up for morning I could hear the buzzing in my head. It was frenetic. She was getting a headful from somebody.

I stared at myself in the mirror and considered what I had just told myself. I already believed she was conversing with somebody through her mind. I could feel the pressure of it. I had overheard some of it. I already believed she was a telepath, despite my denial. Why couldn't I believe the rest?

Because it was absurd. Outer space? No — dealing with aliens was not in my future. Absolutely not. It also didn't explain why she looked the way she did. What, they made her up from a picture? All it did was confuse me and make me want to forget she had ever come into my life. I told my libido to shut up.

She was flat on the floor again while I made breakfast. Grits, which I make really good with cheese and egg, with Spam on the side. Spam tastes about like it sounds. I stopped eating, dissatisfied. I remembered the way I looked in the mirror. I was thirty-six. Christ. When had that happened?

I glanced over at Sharon, who was frowning more

and more deeply. She might be certifiable, but she had broken me out of my dazed and endless grieving. She'd given me the sensation of my body back. I could see that for years I'd been living inside my head, time hardly passing.

I was still as responsible as I'd ever been, but at least I no longer felt that I had to subsist on Spam to make up for it. When the snow cleared I'd go shopping. I'd start reading again, looking for reasons again. Watching the weather go by wasn't going to be enough anymore.

The buzzing stopped. Sharon sat up and rubbed her forehead. "Do you have any pain killers?"

"Sure." I gestured toward the bathroom area. "In the cabinet on the wall. I made you some breakfast."

"Sela wants me to go home," she announced after downing two aspirin. She ate the Spam as if it were filet mignon. "This is really good, by the way. Thank you." She was practically licking the empty bowl of grits.

"Let me guess, there's a special place where you go to be transported around."

She was unamused. "As a matter of fact, yes."

"But it's not too reliable, because you're here and not where you were supposed to be."

"The storm was a higher electrical force than we anticipated. They make good covers but add an element of unpredictability. Retrieval is not as hard."

"Sure," I said amiably. "You'll be needing to go before you violate a prime directive or something."

She leaned across the counter. I found I could not look away. Her gaze bored into the back of my brain.

"There is no Star Trek Federation, there is no prime directive. There is no universal understanding of honor and ethics. I'm here because I belong here, which seems like a good reason to me. But there are other species who are also here — and they're here just because they can be."

I blinked, finally. "I told you to cut that out."

She gave me a pitying look. "What, is that just not nice? Guess what, the universe is full of not nice people. You can't go forward expecting any of them to respect your sensibilities of what is nice."

"I'm not going anywhere." The canyon was as stationary and unchanging as anything could be. Perhaps that was why I loved it so.

"At this very minute you are traveling nearly eight thousand miles every day around a magnetic axis. At the same time you are revolving a million miles a year around a nuclear explosion you can see in your sky. You're traveling every second of your life. Standing still is just an illusion."

"You know what I meant." I was not going to let her confuse me. "I am not going forward with you into some sort of demented reality. You can go swing bones with monkeys around a monolith if you like. I'm staying here."

"All I want," she said stubbornly, "is to find the road out of here."

"What about your top-secret mission? Or did you piss off the boss too much?"

Her lips twitched. "She did comment that contact with humans was making me more human."

"How insulting," I said, with mock outrage. "Say that to a Vulcan and you'll get nerve-pinched."

Her smile turned nasty. "You go right on believing

in powerful, intelligent races, who don't make mistakes and share your sense of honor and morality. It's about as real as Santa Claus."

"Santa Claus exists because we think he does." I could argue this five ways from Sunday thanks to Sartre, Descarte, Kant, et cetera. Who knew it would all come in handy one day?

"Do I exist?"

"Sure," I said, friendly as I could be. "You believe you do, therefore you do. I'm a bit of a Platonic idealist at heart. Though I've often considered Sartre's terrifying freedom in a lonely universe too close to my own experience to ignore." She looked puzzled. "What, no Sartre in your education? First no Dorothy Parker and now this? You don't know everything, do you?"

She sighed heavily. "I don't even know why I care what you believe."

"It's a human failing — we all want to be right."

"No, that's a universal failing. Every being wants to be right."

"Call it what you will." I pointed at the door. "What's outside the door is called snow. You're welcome to walk to Chinle in it, it's twelve miles. Avoid the river, it's wet. Look out for pools created by runoff, those are wet too."

She gave me a look that was clearly meant to reduce me to ashes. Then she threw up her hands. "I don't care. I really don't." She walked to the window and looked out. "Snow is just cold water. I'm used to water." She collected her all-weather gear from behind the stove. "I don't care what you think, and I don't need any help."

"You're sounding more human by the minute." She sounded just like me, in fact. "The lady doth protest too much, methinks." Let her smoke some Shakespeare.

"To be or not to be — that has always been the question for me. It's the only question that matters."

She stripped out of my Princeton sweats, and I felt weak in the knees. I knew exactly who was protesting too much. But what was I going to do about it? Ask her to stay? "You don't know the way."

She closed her eyes, and I felt the invasion — it was nothing like her mind had felt before. The sensation of her search was like a pin probing in my brain, and I couldn't stop it. In two, maybe three heartbeats she was done. It was an eternity.

"I do now," she snapped. She stepped into her all-weather suit and pulled up the zipper.

I just stood there. Of all the things I was struggling so hard not to believe, that she could do that to me with so little regard left me astonished and wounded. After all that she had already done . . . I just couldn't believe it.

"If that was all you wanted," I whispered, "why didn't you just do that when you got here? Why all the rest?"

"Sorry you don't like my methods. But I don't exist except to myself." She fastened the cuffs and walked to the door.

"Why did you make me think you were human?"

She turned from the open door. "I *am* human. That's the whole damn point."

"What you just did to me was not human." My voice trembled. "It was inhuman." I could still feel the violation. "You did it before without asking, and it wasn't right. And you keep doing it, and that's not right. But if you're going to keep doing it, you could at least try to be kind."

"Are humans really kind?"

Images flashed through my mind — sights and sounds I had never seen or heard. What was ethnic cleansing? Who were Matthew Shepard and James Byrd Jr.? A dozen dead children and a teacher killed by two other children in Colorado? Millions displaced, thousands and thousands dead in Kosovo? Had this all happened since I'd turned off the radio and shunned the news?

The roll call of the dead never seemed to end and she was just showing me the last couple of years. My own mind found the Holocaust and atom bombs, the Long March . . . it was too much to bear.

Despair was my constant companion and yet, despite the onslaught of terror and evidence of hate that was consuming me, I found a simple truth that had been there all along. I'd been trying to give up all these years and now that she was proving that life *is* insanity and pain, and nothing, *nothing* happens for a reason, that there could never be a damn good thing from any of our hateful and violent history, I fought back. I hadn't even known that I could.

I know that hate and pain exist, but so does love.

My grandparents loved me. Hosteen Sam loved me. I loved them all. I would have loved Laney if I could have just let myself get on with life. Christa McAuliffe's children and husband loved her.

Even a refugee, running from annihilation of her life, is loved by somebody, or she wouldn't run. Maybe the someone who loves her is just herself. Maybe I clung to the edges of cliffs when I thought I wanted to die because I loved myself.

Love is reason enough to exist.

Love is reason enough to be human, reason enough to fight hate and pain.

Love is reason enough to rise above the past.

Part 2:
Changing Woman

5

The Jeep was close enough to where I had left it for me not to care that it had obviously been borrowed. I was pouring sweat and panting when I scooped the keys off the front seat and got in. Leaving the keys meant no broken windows and a good chance that the desperate person who had come all the way out here to borrow it would be grateful enough to treat it well. Whoever had had it last had even left me a half-tank of gas.

Sharon was out here somewhere. In spite of her determination, I didn't believe she could walk all the way to Chinle without help. She'd left the hogan in tears, her shame reverberating with the slamming door.

It was the sense of shame and horror she had left behind that had got me into hiking clothes. I knew all about shame and horror over your own actions, and I didn't think she was ready to handle the combination. It was potent stuff, and she was already plenty disturbed.

She was human, but from outer space? Right. She was the daughter of a dead woman who wasn't her mother? Right. She was a telepath, but not a very good one? Right. Disturbed was an understatement.

If she was a telepath, then she would take the route I would have taken. If she wasn't, a far more likely scenario, then she was going to get lost. South Rim Drive had numerous places where I could pull close to canyon edge and scan the valley floor for her. This early in the season the cottonwoods weren't blooming, so her bright blue suit would be hard to miss. On the other hand, if she was using the road, I would catch up to her shortly.

My motives, I told myself, were purely altruistic. I knew I was lying to myself, but it was no time for truth. Truth had become irrelevant when coping with Sharon and all she represented.

Fifteen minutes of fairly good speed on the potted road didn't bring her into sight.

I halted on a small rise. The morning sun was hot, as if yesterday's storm was just a mistake. Snow was melting fast, making conditions more muddy than anything else. It was not great for walking. But there was no sign of her. She must still be in the canyon, I thought, perhaps following Chinle Wash and getting soaking wet.

I left the car to climb up a dome of sandstone for a better vantage point. From there I could see that the valley floor was a mess of melting snow and mud. She would have chosen the road if she had any sense. Yeah, but did she have any sense?

I fished in my backpack for binoculars, then scanned the canyon floor for any sign of her bright blue suit. The air was fresh and clear — it had the breath of spring at last. Normally I would have lingered on the fascinating whorls and mounds of varicolored red rock and the way it puddled and sculpted throughout the canyon. The formations looked like the earth's breasts, making the entire canyon female to my way of thinking.

There was no sign of Sharon. I detoured to Sliding Rock Ruin so I could view the valley floor, then pulled off the drive a few more miles ahead where it curved closer to the canyon rim. I couldn't believe she would be that far ahead — it had taken me no more than ten minutes to dress and pack a survival kit. True, if she hiked out directly to the road while I had to backtrack a little to the Jeep, she would have been considerably ahead of me. But there was no way she could be opposite White House Ruin already. I looked anyway.

Of course that was where she was.

I kept my binoculars on her as long as she was in view. She was running along South Rim Drive with the steady, unflagging pace of a marathoner.

I hustled back to the Jeep, feeling foolish and unnecessary. She was already three-quarters of the way to Chinle and looked as if she could run all the way to Flagstaff without pausing. I'd be lucky to catch her at all.

She had a bottle of Coke in one hand and a bag of chips in the other when I pulled into the gas station closest to the canyon entrance. There were two empty water bottles on the bench next to her. She sat there so calmly, looking for all the world like an ordinary hiker taking a break.

I cut the engine and tried to think of a way to talk to her without further embarrassing myself. Nothing came to me. I trudged across the broken asphalt toward her. I knew she sensed me there, but she didn't look my way.

I stood there for a minute, feeling stupid. "That stuff isn't good for you."

She took another long, thirsty swig of the Coke. "But it tastes great." She looked up at me then, grinning. "I was afraid after your coffee tasted so bad that everything would."

"Thanks." I tried to sound hurt, even though my coffee did taste like warmed over mud. "I wasn't sure you had money." I hoped she would think that was why I had chased her all the way out here.

"I brought coins with me. It's amazing what a skilled . . . technician can provide."

"Won't get caught passing counterfeit?"

"Coin is not paper money. Coins have intrinsic value. Besides, they may not have been made in a mint, but there is no way to tell. Silver and nickel are silver and nickel. It's just inconveniently low denominations. And heavy."

I sat down next to her and watched the traffic weaving its way through one of Chinle's few stoplights. The raucous sound of children in the schoolyard injected a moment of normalcy in an otherwise very strange day.

She offered me the chips. As I munched I decided the next words had to be hers.

It was a long wait. She finished the chips and the Coke, studied her boots and finally sighed heavily. "I'm so sorry. It's all I ever seem to say to you."

"I can't say that you should think nothing of it. It wasn't very pleasant on the receiving end. But I can't find any ill will toward you either." I stared at my own boots. "I don't understand much of what you said, and I'm not sure I want to. Maybe you're not of this world, but I believe you're human." I managed to find a wry laugh. "You've fucked up too much not to be."

Her laugh was edged with bitterness. "You don't have any idea what it's like to be odd woman out. Never belonging, not really being able to join in on anything."

"I know only too well."

She looked at me curiously, and I could tell she wanted to look in my mind and find out why. But she didn't, at least not that I could tell. "You mean because you were in such a minority here? Your heritage, your skin?"

"Partly. And partly because I'm — as I think you know — I'm gay."

She blushed, then put her hands to her cheeks in amazement. "Well, that's a foreign sensation." She cleared her throat. "Oh my. So that's embarrassment. I didn't have any experience with that growing up."

"I have to ask. You look to me like you're my age. But you sound like you just got out of school."

"I did just get out of school." She sighed again, but with more humor. "I'm getting tired of being cryptic. Sela is not always right — she's my teacher, my mentor, all that. But she's not always right."

"Nobody ever is. I know that better than anybody."

"Tell that to Sela. Look. You know what it feels like to be one of a few. But I wasn't just in the minority, I was the only one. There wasn't anybody else like me. When you can't share the same air with everyone else, when you can't even touch them —"

"Oh, shit." I took a ragged breath. "I don't want to piss you off, but I just can't believe this."

She put her hand on mine. I could feel her shudder. "You have no idea how welcome this is."

But I do, I wanted to say. Every part of me felt the welcome pleasure of being touched. "I still can't believe what you want me to believe."

Footsteps crunching toward us startled me from the realization that I could never get enough of the feel of her skin.

"Amanda Martin, can that possibly be you?"

I recognized the stooped figure with the graying braids instantly. "Mrs. Beaker! Yeah, it's me."

"Out of that bolt-hole at last. I thought that was your Jeep, but I was sure it was Jimmy Begay driving it again." Mrs. Beaker had run the gas station store since I was a girl. Her light brown eyes were as bright as ever, but her back was even more hunched. Her chin was barely higher than the counter she usually tended in the little store. She looked at Sharon curiously, taking note of our joined hands.

I got up to kiss her withered cheek in greeting. "So Jimmy's the one borrowing it? That's okay — at least it had gas in it. This is Sharon, a friend of mine." I knew Mrs. Beaker heard the hesitation in my voice, but she smiled pleasantly.

Sharon held out her hand to Mrs. Beaker, and I swear I felt her thrill of joy as Mrs. Beaker shook it. I clearly heard her thoughts. :*That makes two.*:

Shit.

"Are you visiting Amanda for long?"

Sharon shook her head. "Actually, I have to head for home."

"That's a shame — you had the worst of our weather. It'll be pleasant for the next week at least."

Sharon hesitated slightly. "I'm out of vacation time."

Mrs. Beaker nodded knowingly. "A vacation, that's what I've been needing all my life. See the Grand Canyon some day."

Sharon stood up suddenly, startling me. Mrs. Beaker had to look up. "I have a little bit of . . . experience with back trouble." She carefully put her hands behind her. "I would love to give you a short backrub. I bet you'll feel like a million bucks."

Mrs. Beaker gave Sharon a long look. It was probably Sharon's puppylike eagerness to please, and the way she was so clearly waiting for explicit permission, that made her say, "That sounds like a fine idea."

Sharon had Mrs. Beaker sit beside her on the bench, then she slowly raised her hands, as if expecting a protest any moment. When none came, she put both hands lightly on Mrs. Beaker's shoulders.

Mrs. Beaker's eyes closed, then a surprised smile lit her lined face. Sharon was flushed with concentration, and her hands never moved.

After a minute, maybe two, Sharon lifted her hands and Mrs. Beaker straightened up, then stood. She stood taller than I'd ever seen her in all my life. Habitual lines of pain had eased from her face.

She stammered amazed thanks to Sharon, who made little of what she had done. "It's just a little trick with nerve pressure points. It'll last a while, though." I could tell Sharon had no evil intent, but I could also tell she was lying about something.

"Your clan has a powerful medicine animal," Mrs. Beaker said. She was hunching and shaking her shoulders as if making up for lost time. She pulled a heavy silver ring from her little finger. "This is my medicine ring, a gift from my *kinaalda* — my changing woman sing, too many years ago to count. Please take it. I have no daughter or granddaughter to give it to. I have never wished to part with it, but now it jumps from my finger. The medicine is yours." She curled Sharon's hand around the ring and nodded, as if well pleased.

"I can't take your ring," Sharon protested. "It was nothing —"

"Nothing to the wind does not mean nothing to me." Mrs. Beaker was sounding just like Hosteen Sam. "It was on my mind where I should leave it. I have made small medicine in my time, and I can't let someone think it's ordinary. If anyone should ask, tell them you have made a great friend with Born for Water."

My eyebrows went up as far as they could go. Mrs. Beaker might mention her clan affiliation around me, but Sharon was an outsider. Something passed be-

tween them that was less tangible than thought —
well, at least I couldn't discern what it was.

Then their hands separated and Sharon had the
ring. She slipped it onto the same finger Mrs. Beaker
had worn it on. It didn't surprise me that it fit. With
a final nod and a kiss on my cheek, Mrs. Beaker went
back into the market.

Sharon beamed while tears swam in her eyes. It
was like looking into liquid topaz. "That was
amazing." She glanced down at the ring, and I
realized I had been holding my breath. "We are so
wrong about you."

Telepath. Healer. Human. My knees were wobbly,
but I could hear, faintly inside me, the happy sound of
singing.

She led the way to the Jeep, scrambling into the
passenger side as if I'd asked her to. I got behind the
wheel, then looked over at her. I felt as if the Jeep
was suspended in time, in space. Beliefs as certain as
gravity had fled me. What I had just seen, all I had
experienced — I could finally let myself believe.

She put her hand, heavier now with the ring, on
mine. *:Everything is going to be fine.:*

:How can you be so sure?: I knew I had just
entered a reality I had never conceived. I felt the
change so profoundly that when I glanced outside I
expected the sky to be purple or green, the road to be
orange, the puffs of cloud yellow or red. "How could
something so astonishing happen to just me?"

"I ask myself the same thing. The last twenty-four
hours haven't been easy, but I still wonder — how did
I get to be so lucky?"

I smiled ruefully. "Lucky enough to have a mad-
woman take you in, make you sleep in a chair, nearly

choke you to death?" My hand was hot where she touched it, and every nerve was singing with life.

She reached over to stroke my cheek with her other hand. "Lucky enough to feel the press of human flesh, to glimpse unexpected depths of emotion. Because of you I am beginning to understand what it means to be alive."

My lips nuzzled her fingertips. *:Because of you, I am remembering what it means to be alive.:*

Belief or disbelief — all my questions were irrelevant. All that mattered was the warmth of her lips and the ringing joy that swept through me. I'd lived in the cold for so long. She was warming the darkest parts of my soul with generous light, and I did not want her to stop kissing me.

A blast from a truck on the highway separated us. There were several amused people standing around the Jeep, checking their watches. One of the men shouted, "Six minutes! And that's just since I got here." The others applauded. I glanced at the store doorway and saw Mrs. Beaker clapping as well.

I had had no sensation of time passing, but it obviously must have. I could have kissed her for eternity and never noticed the passage of a single minute.

Sharon was adorable all red, and I knew my face was a match for hers. I waved with a poor attempt at serenity and got us the hell out of there. I instinctively headed north on 191 toward the grocery store and Chinle's small business area.

"I would love to have a cheeseburger," Sharon said as the golden arches flashed by us.

I was reeling from a kiss that surpassed sex and she was thinking about her stomach.

Sharon was blushing again. "Well, I'm hungry. That stuff we had for breakfast was great, but it was a long time ago."

"If you think Spam is tasty, then I suppose a cheeseburger will be heavenly."

We devoured our lunch in the parking lot with the windows down. The sun was glorious. To the east the sky was filled with Georgia O'Keeffe clouds — cotton puffs dotted against high-country blue.

Sharon licked secret sauce from her fingers and looked hungrily at my leftover French fries. "Go for it," I said.

She sat back happily with the bag on her lap. "I could get to like this."

I laughed. "Fast food and my cooking — they're nothing to judge cuisine by. And they're not really good for you."

"It appears that numerous things that aren't good for me are irresistible." She was staring at the French fries, but her mind, ever so gently, brushed mine with an unmistakable caress.

I tried to hide my responsive shudder. "How do you know I'm not good for you?"

"I don't want to go home. Sela is freaking out — she wants to talk in the worst way."

"You can shut her out?"

Her chipmunk cheeks were in full display. "Yeah, apparently I can. Nobody told me I'd be able to do that."

"So you don't have to go home."

"That thought had crossed my mind. I don't want to talk about it, though. You're entirely too much like Eve, and your world is a great big apple."

I slurped the last of my chocolate shake. "You're

not falling for that old line about women being responsible for all evil and the downfall of God's perfection, are you?"

"That story does not play well where I come from, believe me. It's one of the reasons we weren't sure how to . . . evaluate your culture."

"You have equality of the sexes?"

"Well . . . not exactly." Sharon's evasion didn't fool me one bit.

"Judge not, lest ye be judged, honey."

"Okay — you're right. I can't very well judge what men have done to women when we haven't even had the problem to deal with."

I frowned. "Wait a minute — male society in general has treated women pretty poorly. That's easy to judge."

"But you told me not to!"

"Well, you were sounding all superior, as if your people would never succumb to such a thing as sexism."

"Well, we wouldn't. I mean we can't. Where I'm from we don't have two sexes. There's just one."

I blinked. "Cool." For a moment I contemplated about a world without any men at all, not even the good ones. "I think. Maybe."

"There are maker races all over the galaxy. You're one of them, and so are the people where I'm from. I think the makers did a little experimenting. You have two sexes, we have one, others have three. The universe defaults to diversity."

We were getting into troubled waters for me. "You know that I believe you, but I'm not ready to believe in the rest of it. Not yet." I took a deep breath. "It gives me a headache."

"I think you're entitled to feel — what's the word? — shell-shocked?"

Shell-shocked didn't even begin to cover it. "If you're human, what are they?" I don't think I had, in any nightmare or dream, ever supposed that I would ask that question of anyone.

She sighed. "I'm not supposed to tell. Of course I'm not supposed to have told you any of what I've said so far. There was no way to prepare me for this."

"It's a little too late to turn back the clock."

She opened her mouth as if she had an answer to that, then closed it again. She ate another fry, then said, "There are no English sounds for the name of where I'm from. All communication is thought. Using the voice is considered in bad taste for anything but singing and ritual. They've settled on the name *Pallas* for their world and *Pallasians* for themselves when they make contact. Which they'll do when they think the time is right." She paused. "I said *they*, didn't I?"

I nodded.

"It's amazing what a change in perspective can do. Until today, *we* meant them and me. *They* meant you guys." She looked at her hands, and I sensed the wrench it took for her to change her thinking. "Pallasians look very much like . . . us. I mean, women."

"Show me."

We shared a look that made the air between us hot. "Are you sure?"

"Yes." I swallowed hard. I needed to believe.

When her thoughts wrapped themselves inside me they were enhanced by a definite physical pleasure. I remembered the way I had relived being with Laney and knew that Sharon had made it real for me.

Instead of embarrassment, I felt only wonder. Yes, she had hurt me deliberately, and yes she had taken me to places I desperately wanted to forget. But I invited her now, and I needed to know if I could trust her.

She showed me a sunrise in a sky of coral, over red oceans and deep green mountains. I saw it all through her eyes, from a high window. For a moment I was caught in her memories of that place — sometimes happy, sometimes angry, but always feeling like a caged animal. It was a horrible feeling.

:*How did you survive it?*:

:*My other option was death. I was not that desperate, not yet. I was loved.*:

A woman turned to look at me, her skin a delicate orange, eyes deeply blue with whites ever so faintly pink. Her hair was pure white. Aside from her skin she could have been a neighbor or someone's mother. She gestured at me in Sharon's memory, and I saw that her fingers were much longer than mine — an extra joint made them seem incredibly elegant.

:*Sela.*:

I wondered what her skin and hair felt like, what the air smelled like, how the sun would feel beating down on me.

:*I don't know those things. If I was going to walk in their atmosphere they would have had to change me permanently. I would have never been able to come here. When I go back, they'll change me then. I get to experience both my worlds that way.*:

I avoided the topic of her going back. :*Are all of them so lovely?*:

She withdrew from my mind, and the sensation made my thighs clench. I was mixing the mental and physical far too readily.

"From what I've seen of the universe, they are particularly lovely." She added softly, "Human women are beautiful too."

I tried to lighten things up. It seemed necessary at that moment. "For a lesbian like me, a planet of lovely, intelligent women sounds like paradise."

"Yes, well, having only the one choice means we are all lesbians, I suppose."

I chuckled. "I'm just wondering what the politically correct set would say. You don't have a choice to be lesbians, so are you really lesbians?"

Sharon snorted. "Does the distinction of having a choice matter?"

I gazed at her lips. :*Not to me.*: Speaking to her with my mind was getting easier. I could paint the words with emotions too subtle for my voice.

"Stop that," she said unconvincingly. "You make it hard to think."

:*Thinking is not what's on my mind.*:

"Cut that out! I'm serious. Which reminds me — I think you and I can do that because you're a lesbian."

"Really? Lesbians have some sort of telepathy gene?"

"How the hell should I know?" Sharon rolled her eyes. "What I know is that a Pallasian was here before. Actually on Earth. It was an accident, and she made mind contact with lesbians. No one knows if that was a fluke. Someday I'll tell you the whole story about the explorer. In part, that's why I'm here."

"But it doesn't seem to be a fluke right now, does it?"

:*Right now it seems like a blessing.*: The mental caress was plain in its meaning.

I swallowed hard. "For someone who's telling me

to stop, you're indulging way too much. It's a long way back to the hogan." Yesterday afternoon she'd been naked and I hadn't bothered to look. Now I wanted to unzip her suit with my tongue.

"I have obligations," she said with a gratifying amount of reluctance. "No matter what happens later, I have things I must do. I have messages for the women who helped the explorer. One has some urgency."

"I know the way to L.A. Turn right at Flagstaff, then ask, no problem. I wish I'd packed a suitcase, though."

"That would be so wonderful," she whispered. A tiny smile parted her lips. "That is, if you don't have any other plans."

I hadn't had any plans for thirteen years. I laughed and started the Jeep. "I'll clear my calendar."

"Have your people call my people." Sharon giggled like a child.

I had no right to feel so lighthearted. "Before we go, there is someone I have to see. Someone I want you to meet."

6

Hosteen Sam lived in a small ranch style house south of the three motels that sat outside the canyon entrance. Canyon de Chelley National Monument drew a number of tourists in spite of its remote location. As we passed the motels, I seriously considered pulling into one. Just an hour, I thought. I could do so much with her in a single hour.

"If we stopped we wouldn't leave for days." Sharon sounded very final about it, but I noticed she looked longingly at the Vacancy signs as we passed.

I sighed. An hour was just a quickie, anyway. A real shower with shampoo sounded almost as good. It had been eons since I'd cared about either activity.

I gave myself a stern lecture. If a shower sounded as good as sex, my priorities were seriously out of whack. Thirteen years I'd given up in pursuit of regret, and I had nothing to show for it except a body I hardly recognized. The self-denial and years spent researching, reading, crying — they'd changed nothing. What a monumental display of self-pity, I thought.

"Don't regret it," Sharon said. "You were there when I needed you." I glowered at her. "You're broadcasting again," she said. "I can't help it."

I seriously doubted that Sharon needed me, but it was nice to hear. "I'll try not to, but you have to tell me when I'm doing it or I'll never learn."

"It'd be easier to tell you when you're not."

I mimicked her words to my reflection in the rearview mirror. Sharon playfully smacked my hand. I tried to warn myself that I was far too comfortable with her, but it was easy to ignore the little voice.

I hadn't seen or heard from Hosteen Sam for about three months. He was increasingly frail of body, but I hoped to find him well. When I stopped in front of the small house, Sharon began to open her door. I stopped her with a gentle touch on her arm.

"Navajo custom. Wait to see if we're welcome."

Since I had no reason to think he was not home — it was between seasons for any of the large ceremonial sings he normally presided over — I waited with no concerns. After about two minutes, his door opened and the bandy-legged figure I'd loved for most of my life came into view. He waved a plain greeting, and I scrambled out of the car.

"Hosteen Sam!" His embrace was as strong as always, though his shoulders seemed thinner than ever. His dense, gray braids were as usual dotted with bits of feather down from his constant working with ceremonial masks and headdresses. "I am so glad to see you!"

"Little Red, you are a pleasure for an old man's eyes. I've been expecting you."

I was in the mood to believe in magic. "Which animal spirit told you I was coming?"

"Spirit of bell," he said with great seriousness.

"You don't believe in spirits in bells." His extreme gravity meant he was teasing me.

"Telephone bell. Edna Beaker said you might bring someone to meet me." He looked pointedly at Sharon.

I made a face at the way he had pulled my leg and turned to Sharon. "Hosteen Sam Nakai, this is Sharon . . ." I stumbled, realizing I had no last name for her. With a flash of thought, she told me. "Sharon Cauliffe."

"Welcome, Sharon Cauliffe." He never took his piercing gaze from her.

"I'm honored to meet you. Amy has told me so much about you."

Her use of the nickname I'd forbidden anyone he knew of to use raised Hosteen Sam's eyebrows. I wondered if Mrs. Beaker had called him before or after the kiss Sharon and I had shared.

Not knowing made me blush. Hosteen Sam smiled knowingly, the old coot. He'd heard all about the kiss.

We were settled with large glasses of Hosteen Sam's legendary lemonade before any subject not related to family and friends could be broached. We sipped a little longer, and Hosteen Sam finished telling me about his sister's newest grandchild. Then he turned his gray-brown eyes on Sharon.

"You are very young to have such powerful medicine."

"I'm about Amy's age," she said. I loved hearing her say my name that way.

"That is very young to an old man."

Sharon gazed at him for a long moment, then observed, "You are very young for old man."

This statement pleased him inordinately. "I am a young man in an old body. Little Red makes me remember her grandmother when I was a young man in a young man's body."

"I'll tell you a secret," Sharon said. "When I was young, I was old. Now that I'm older, I feel very young."

I sighed. They were like peas in a pod, the two of them. Talking in circles and riddles and understanding each other very well. Hosteen Sam and my grandmother had talked that way too. I never knew what the heck was going on.

"How long have you known Little Red?"

Sharon didn't blink. "About twenty-four hours, give or take an hour or so."

He turned his head to regard me. I squirmed. Kissing her in public after knowing her for less than a day? "I picked her up out of the canyon mud yesterday."

Sharon tsked at me. "It was the other way around.

She came to my rescue, and I picked *her* up out of the mud."

"Little Red has always been impetuous."

I started to defend myself, then realized he was absolutely right. I'd known Sharon for only a day, and I already believed she was from a planet called Pallas, could heal with her hands, practiced telepathy regularly and was an incredible kisser. Well, I didn't *believe* she was a good kisser, I knew that for a fact, but that was beside the point. The point, I told myself, was that it hadn't exactly been a typical day and I was far too sanguine about the whole matter.

"I mean it in a modest way when I say I am not an ordinary woman," Sharon was saying seriously. "I am as I was made."

"Edna Beaker assured me you were far from ordinary." He glanced at me again, as if I shouldn't necessarily be privy to his next question. "How long have you had medicine?"

"I — it's in my genetics."

"Family medicine can be powerful."

I was puzzled. If Sharon was so human, how could she have a talent like healing? And telepathy? And why hadn't I thought of that little question sooner?

"It's not so much medicine as working with what is there. I can't create anything or make anything go away. I can just rearrange things."

How exactly did a so-called human have such an ability? The more she talked, the more troubled I became. Hosteen Sam was right — I was too impulsive. Too trusting.

Hosteen Sam was answering Sharon's question about the function of spirit animals. "They can provide guidance or trickery, depending on their mood. One should never take spirit guides for granted."

"That makes sense," Sharon said. "I don't think I have a spirit animal, though."

"We do not have spirit animals," Hosteen Sam said, with a mischievous twinkle. "They have us."

"I perceive the difference." Sharon nodded as if everything made perfect sense.

I didn't believe in spirit animals and medicine bundles, no more than I believed in resurrections and immaculate conceptions. Why did I believe in Sharon? I puzzled it over while the two of them continued their oblique conversation.

Hosteen Sam had not asked, but Sharon was holding one of his hands between hers. She was frowning. "I'm sorry, but there's little I can do. I can soften it, make it less brittle so there's less abrasion against your ligaments. But I can't make it go away, or settle somewhere else in your body less painful. Mrs. Beaker had trapped soft tissue, that was simple to distribute." She smiled sadly. "I've never dealt with arthritis before."

More half-truths, I thought. She'd never dealt with any human ailments but her own.

Hosteen Sam liked Sharon very much. He was never wrong about people. It made me want to trust her, but my doubts were redoubling by the minute.

As we left, Sharon went ahead. I lingered a moment to embrace him.

"You have made a good choice, Little Red. Happiness Girl suits you."

"I've only known her a day," I said stubbornly. "I'm hardly Long Life Boy to her Happiness Girl."

"Does the wind bow to time? Happiness Girl and

Long Life Boy make Changing Woman. You will see that I am right."

It was impossible to argue with him. "I haven't chosen anything."

"Time will tell. Speaking of time, do not stay away so long. I will not live forever."

"Are you ill?" I examined his face carefully, but he seemed much the same as the last time I saw him.

"Your amazing friend politely chose not to say what doctors have said. Did you not hear her urge me to go riding again, even if I'm stiff for a week?"

I had heard, but apparently not understood Sharon had meant he should ride while he still could. "I'll come back soon. I think I may be at the end of needing the hogan. I'll find some place in town." Living anywhere else was still inconceivable.

He nodded knowingly. "She managed in a day what I could not do in years. She is not an ordinary woman."

"You two got along entirely too well."

"You can't blame an old man for flirting, Little Red. If I'd flirted more as a young man, you might have been my granddaughter-in-fact."

He was inside his house before I closed my mouth.

I drove back into the canyon instead of to the grocery store. There were a few tourists at the off-the-road overlooks, so I passed them up in favor of the short, tourist-daunting road to the Sliding Rock Ruin overlook. I had too many questions to go with her without some answers, and I didn't want any distractions.

"You're troubled."

Sharon had rightly read my mood. "You haven't told me everything. Like how you're human, but you have all these extra abilities."

"I didn't think you wanted to know."

"I think I have to." I killed the engine and turned to face her. "Why do you look like her? How do you do the things you do?" I swallowed hard. "What exactly are you?"

"I'm ninety-six percent human. It's the ninety-six percent that counts. How I breathe, how I eat, how I respond to things. Before yesterday, I was deeply familiar with anger and resentment, with contentment and gratitude. Intellectual curiosity and seeking to understand something just because it's there — that was my life. I hated it sometimes. Sometimes I thought it wasn't fair for them to keep me."

Urgency made me hoarse. "Where did you come from?"

"Let me finish — I need to tell you why. Why I'm the way I am, making such a mess of things mostly because I've never done anything but think in my whole life. Thinking isn't everything. You cannot think the touch of another hand. You can't think snow on your fingertips." She wiped away a tear that trickled down one cheek. "I've never cried before, certainly never kissed before."

My jaw quivered. I wanted not to care about the answers anymore. I wanted not to be troubled by what she was that was more than human. She was real and I wanted her, why couldn't it be that simple?

"In spite of all the media I watched to learn

languages and what humans are like, I never guessed what desire could be." She gasped back a sob. "I didn't understand pleasure and regret, and I thought heartbreak was just poetic license."

"I'll try not to break your heart."

"You can't protect me from myself, from breaking my own heart."

"We'll be fine." I wound my fingers with hers. For that one perfect moment, I believed that everything would be fine, just as she promised.

Sharon's voice was low, and she stumbled over her words as if she could not hold them back any longer. "Maybe someday I'll be able to explain how she did it, but the important fact is that it was done. In those two minutes and forty-five seconds, Sela made a decision. It was the first time you had chosen an ordinary person to go into space. All who went before were your brave and strong, brilliant minds or politicians. Christa was ordinary by comparison, but to be chosen out of so many — she wasn't just one person with extraordinary capabilities. She represented the finest that *any* of you could be. She was just a teacher, an everyday kind of person."

"That's why her death haunts me. She didn't belong up there."

Sharon squeezed my hand. I looked into her eyes and could not look away, not because she held me there, but because they were the only anchors to reality I had.

Sharon was never more earnest. "But she did belong there. There are a lot of species in space. And not one of them got there by following pilots and politicians. You can only be at home in space if you bring all of your people there. We never dreamed you were ready for that step. And there she was — a very human, very ordinary woman carrying the collective hopes and dreams of your world inside her. So Sela . . . preserved the DNA of someone who best represented your potential."

"DNA," I echoed stupidly. She had mentioned it before. I had already absorbed so much that I didn't think I could handle what she was going to say. What I already knew she was going to say. "Oh my God. What exactly did she do to Christa?"

"Nothing Christa was ever aware of. A microscopic, living DNA sample. She didn't want to — and couldn't — take anything more. It was enough to make me. For me to survive even in isolation, they added one more pair of chromosomes to the DNA strand. So they could talk to me."

I pulled my hand free. I found the right word. "Clone. You're Christa's clone. You're her daughter, but she's not your mother." I started to gasp for breath. Words like *abomination* and *beast, hocho* and *skinwalker* — they swelled up in me. I crossed myself and wished I had holy pollen for protection. I covered my mouth, but I could not stop my gasping nor my whimpers of terror. I didn't know what she was anymore — and I had wanted her. I still wanted her. I had let her into my most private and protected places.

Sharon tried to touch me, but I slapped away her hands. I was going to be sick.

"I'm sorry," she said, then I felt the pressure of her mind. It was intolerable.

I pushed my door open so fast I fell out. She was coming around the Jeep to help me, but I couldn't let her touch me. Gasping, I scrabbled under the seat for the tire iron. When she touched my shoulder I came up swinging.

The force of the blow spun her around. She fell and didn't get up.

7

The blood that seeped from the purpling wound in her face was red. Her eyelids were veined with blue. She looked human. She was as vulnerable as a human. She was lying on her side in the mud, and I couldn't tell if she was breathing. I wanted to help her, but my feet wouldn't move. I sat with my back against the Jeep and held on to the tire iron as if it was a life preserver, caught between hope and horror, between belief and revulsion.

Was this what Christa had died for? To bring another kind of being into life? To bring that being, that woman, for me to hold and believe in? No, I could not believe it was part of some grand design. Nothing happens for a reason. If we can make a reason for the bad that happens — countless philosophers say that is good. But who was I to take the good?

Life exists because stars died. Their exploded dust became us, her and me and all I had ever loved and ever hated and everything I would never even know or touch.

When I finally moved I was numb from the cold mud and my hunched position. I crawled the few feet to her side, fear battling with hope. She was alive. I was so glad, and I was so afraid it was another minute or two before I could touch her.

The left side of her face was purple and black where it wasn't bloody. The tire iron had caught her on her cheekbone just below her temple. I put my hand on her other cheek.

:Sharon, wake up. Please.:

I caught a tendril of her thought, random and drifting. I closed my eyes and followed it, hoping to find consciousness. Bursts of music too beautiful to comprehend were mixed with a desperate loneliness — there was Sela, saying no yet again to this mission that Sharon was finally undertaking. Sela was angry and worried, I could see her face lined with anxiety.

:What has happened to Sharon? Where is she?:

I was so surprised that I just stared.

Sela gestured helplessly. :You have enough ability to

talk to me and how you learned to do that I don't want to know. I just want to know where Sharon is. I know she is near you.:

:She's hurt.: I couldn't help but think of the sickening moment the tire iron had struck her.

:What did you do to her? Why?:

:I was terrified out of my mind. I'm frightened by what she is, by you, by all of this.: There was no room for equivocation with Sela. Her mental touch was as firm and piercing as Sharon's was hesitant and gentle. *:But I'm more scared that I've killed her. Please help me.:*

Sela put her face in her hands. *:By all the mother's stars, how could this go so badly?:*

:It doesn't matter right now. Blame it all on me. But she's going to die.:

For one horrible moment, I knew that Sela was thinking that that might be for the best. But when she looked at me again, with eyes of an incredibly deep blue, her face was crumpled with grief. *:She came this far. I can't let it end this way.:*

A brilliant flash of light left me gasping. My hair literally stood up on end as a wave of energy surged through every cell in my body. It was like being struck by lightning without. Sharon convulsed, then began coughing. Her eyes opened. The right eye fixed on me, but the left, surrounded by swelling, was far too dilated.

:Sharon, stay awake, you have to help yourself. Or I'll take you to the doctor in Chinle. It's a long way to a hospital. So try . . . try to help yourself.:

Sharon's lips moved, then her eyes rolled back.

Soothing and low, Sela began to sing. It was a song without words, but I immediately thought of a lazy summer afternoon in a cottonwood tree, listening to water trickle in the river while a bee hummed near my ear. I gently raised Sharon's hands to her face.

:*Please, help yourself. You can do it.*:

My hands were on top of hers, and I tried to will her all my strength. My mind rippled with fractalized images of bone and nerves. I stared at blood, then cells of blood, then I was in the cell, swimming with microorganisms. I fell through the cell into a comet's tail — the stuff of stars was all around me in ever smaller pieces that were still entire universes. With a snap, I found myself around a sliver of bone that lifted and settled back into place, then cells that knitted the severed edges came home again and bonded with their neighbors. Little by little the damage was mended, swollen tissues drained and nerves released from painful pressure.

The work was as delicate as sand painting, grain by grain coaxed into place. My hands felt as if they were deeply inside her, then merely resting on hers. My vision left behind the intricate weaving of tissue and capillaries, and I was looking through my eyes again.

Sela's singing faded away. :*Sharon, tell me you are healed.*:

:*My body is fine.*: She said more to Sela, but I was suddenly too exhausted to stay in the link. I sat back in the mud and concentrated on breathing.

"Amy."

I looked up in a daze. The sun had shifted me into shade. Sharon was standing over me, holding out her hand.

The fear was still there. I had to choose again.

With a flash of insight, I saw that it was easy to

pick despair and anger and hate once and never have to pick again. But hope and love have to be chosen over and over or their remarkable powers fade. "I hate you" lasts forever. "I love you" has to be said every day to have meaning and strength.

I took her hand. I knew I would have to take her hand every day for a very long time or we would never find a way to put the past behind us.

We were as filthy as we had been yesterday, soaked through with mud and freezing. The Jeep's heater did little to warm us, and Sharon echoed my longing thoughts of hot showers and a warm, soft bed.

For a long time she didn't say anything. Words, in a way, were unnecessary. She knew with certainty how sorry I was and that I would not ever be that frightened of her again. Words would not convince her that she shouldn't be afraid of anyone else who would react the way I had. A lot of people would act the same way. Human beings were champions at destroying what they did not understand and therefore feared.

I was too tired to think about secrecy and finding a way for Sharon to stay here — I had no intention of letting her go. The clerk at the motel looked at me with distaste, but my cash was acceptable.

I was really wishing I had packed a change of clothes. It just hadn't occurred to me that I would very likely need one. Getting back into damp clothing would be unpleasant to say the least.

Sharon unzipped her suit, and I forgot about clothing. There was time to worry about mundane details later.

She caught me looking. The slight pinkness that had lingered after she'd healed her face was gone. All that was left was the way she looked at me.

It was terrifying in a completely familiar way. I felt just the way I had the first time I'd had sex. The other woman had been a friend of a friend at Bible college. All the minutes leading up to the moment her fingertips had brushed my body with unmistakable desire had been the most frightening thing that had ever happened to me. I'd found the courage to whisper, "Yes."

Sharon stepped out of the full-length suit, and my mouth was not the only thing that watered. I felt cheap, for just a moment, to want sex so badly with someone I'd known for such a short time, but I reminded myself it had been thirteen years since I'd cared about what I did with my body. Given all that Sharon and I knew of each other it was hardly anonymous. And what if it was? Our desire was mutual.

Her gaze on me was as intimate as a caress, as purposeful as a kiss. I was flushed as I started to take off my own mud-soaked clothes. I heard her breath catch when I pulled my sweatshirt over my head. I piled my clothes on the vanity and in the sink and turned on the shower while every inch of my skin felt the heat of her desire.

The hot water was blissful, but the shower was too small and antiquated to provide much ambiance for a romantic interlude. It was a good thing that neither of us had romance on our minds. The kind of sex I was yearning for didn't require soft candlelight and a sunken tub.

Shampooing each other's hair was an excuse to touch. Fingers slipped down faces, tangled in lips and teeth that crushed them aside in our haste to taste each other. She bit my lower lip, and I spluttered on water, but our gasping, hungry kisses made me yet again lose all sense of time. I pinned her against the shower wall and explored her breasts and ribs. My hand easily slid down her shampoo-slicked abdomen. I might have forgotten how potently pleasurable the touch of a woman was, but my fingers had not forgotten what to do. This is the way women feel, I thought, wet and hot and strong and wanting. It's the way I feel.

Her cry of response was muffled in my shoulder as my fingers slipped over her tight and sensitive places. This part of her was as real and human as it was possible to be. "Get inside me, please, Amy," had no need of telepathy to make me believe she wanted me to take her. Her skin, her mouth, her tongue and her tears were as human and as female as my own, as desirable and intoxicating as any woman I'd ever held.

Our tears mingled — I cried because we both wanted it so much and every sensation was almost unbearable in its pleasure. I cried because she was real and imperfect and conflicted and too hard on herself. Like me, in so many ways, just a human being muddling through circumstances and trying hard to do the right thing and failing most of the time. I cried because she felt so good against me and it had been such a long time since I'd felt good about anything.

We both moaned as she frantically guided my fingers into her. The water was turning cold, but we couldn't stop now. She shuddered and kissed me with bruising force. Her shoulders were hard against me, and one leg was wrapped around both of mine. We were climbing together, moment by moment, toward rapture, toward the instant when we were something more than human. Our spirits swirled like the dust of stars, excited and beautiful and forever driving toward an instant of completion, a flare of passion followed by darkness made intimate for having been warmed by our light.

"Amy," she breathed. I tasted my name on her lips as she kissed me yet again. We were separating more than physically, and I didn't want to lose the feeling of having a part of her spirit meshed with my own.

"That was just the beginning," I whispered. The water was getting too cold to ignore. I turned it off, then wrapped her in a towel, using it to pull her after me toward the bed.

She moved drunkenly, and her mouth looked as bruised as mine felt. "I don't know what could be more —"

"No talking," I said. I pressed her down onto the sheets and took my time exploring her hands, her arms, every inch of her face with kisses and flicks of my tongue. My mouth was so hungry for her skin.

I rolled her on her side and spooned against her back. My lips grazed the nape of her neck while my hand cupped the weight and size of each breast. Her legs were moving against mine, and I teased her with my hand sliding the length of her back to brush between her legs. Her hand joined mine and she tried to draw me inside her again, but I untangled my fingers and went back to my deliberate exploration of her body.

Every inch was human. My teeth nipped at her ribs, then her hip. I pulled her to her back again and I straddled her so my mouth and hands could equally smooth, caress, excite and torment her breasts. Her sighs and whispers were beyond music. I cupped her face in my hands and kissed her desperate mouth, realizing that I was reveling in my control — for once I knew better than she what was needed.

She panted against my mouth, and I abruptly felt her hand finding its way between me and her stomach. She was in me before I knew I did not want to protest — God, it felt so good. She looked up at me, eyes dulled by hunger.

I saw myself reflected there, my need, driving myself down on her fingers. She was half sitting up now, her teeth and lips pleasuring my aching nipples. We were locked in a moment of struggle with ourselves and each other. I wanted what she was doing to me, and I wanted to finish tasting her body. She was intent on being in me, bringing me to ecstasy, but her legs were open in anticipation of my mouth and tongue.

With a gasp of loss and want, I twisted away from her. I caught the hand that had been in me and brought it to my breast while I folded myself around her legs and tasted her at last.

She was trembling as I drank her in. I inhaled her frenzied passion and fed my long-starved energy with the power of her desire as I satisfied both of our very human, very real passions.

I was gasping for breath when she said, in a low, urgent voice, "That was just the beginning."

I was on my back at last, and she was over me, her eyes as penetrating as the fingers I welcomed again. Determination made her movements certain, and she could have no doubt how much I wanted her. She stared into my eyes, watched my face mirror every stroke. I gave myself completely to the wild pleasure of her mouth when it finally captured me. There was no gravity to keep me on the bed, only her mouth kept me from floating in stars.

I was sweating and exhausted when time seemed to begin again. It was dark outside, but I had no concept of how late or early it might be.

She stirred against me. "That was just the beginning."

"I don't think I can move." I was serious.

:Don't move. Close your eyes:

She began with colors in shades I did not have enough names for — coral, salmon, peach and more. A brilliant pink was suffused with rose and became crimson, then darkened to fathomless black. The stars came out and a faceless moon peered over a red horizon, tinted with the most delicate mauve.

The moon's light wrapped around me then seemed to come from within me. I floated in time, and a thousand voices joined in a song that made my nerves burn. I did not understand the words, but my body knew the rhythm and the melody — life is exultation and love is life's most potent coin.

:I am stars, I am enraptured sky.:

Her thoughts were like a breeze caressing each leaf it stirred. I was a thousand leaves, a thousand feathers, all lifted and touched by the hint of her thought.

:*Remember . . . skin, wet, lips, shoulders . . . remember.*:

I was kissing the crook of Laney's arm, necking with a girl in the library, fumbling my way through my first kiss. All of my sexualness was swirling in my head and through my body. I smelled leather and stale bar smoke and old books, and each had the reminder of a woman and the way she touched me.

My body was consumed with heat. Then I felt Sharon's hands on my breasts. It was a gentle touch that echoed through my body, into my thoughts, then surged to her thoughts, which were awash with the sensation of touching me.

:*You are stars. You spread yourself on the sky.*:

We were mirrors of sensation, a hundred iterations of my body with her body with my body with her mind with my mind — radiant stars burning all they touched with a white hot passion that resounded in each other. I did not know where I stopped and she began. There was an eternity between every heartbeat, and we illuminated the darkness.

:*We are stars . . . we are sky . . . we are . . .*:
:*. . . the wind . . . we are one.*:

I think too much.
:*What's wrong?*:
I sighed. The sun was coming up — our second

116

sunrise. Every part of my body and mind felt as if it had been individually blessed and brought to its own personal orgasm. The feeling faded the longer I was awake and the more I thought. My growling stomach did not help.

"I'm afraid of the way I'm going to feel when I see you."

"Embarrassed? Shy?" She snuggled a little closer to me, all warmth and softness.

I couldn't find an easy way to say it. "I'm afraid that when I see you I'll feel like I slept with my best friend's mother." I knew that Sharon was not Christa, and that Christa was dead. I knew that there had never been the slightest hint that Christa was not heterosexual, which just proved that the woman I had had sex with could not be Christa. I was still afraid that when I saw her again my stomach would feel that same lurch of impossibility and dismay.

Sharon put her cheek against my shoulder. "I'm afraid that when I look in the mirror I won't know who I am. I am not Sela's creation, I am not Christa, and I'm not her daughter. I don't know why I'm here."

In my desire to comfort her, I said the wrong thing. "You sound very human."

"But I'm not human!"

She was out of bed and on her feet before I could say more than, "You know what I mean!"

She flipped on a light. My stomach flip-flopped because I felt like I'd just slept with my best friend's mother and I wanted to do it again.

"I have no right to this body," she said.

I wanted every inch of that body.

"Sela had no right to do what she did. I'm an experiment, an academic exercise, and I will cause too many people too much pain."

"I got over it," I said.

"After you nearly killed me." She saw me flinch. "I'm sorry," she said quickly. "I'm not trying to make you feel bad again."

"I know." I did believe her. "I'm not really a violent person — and look at my peaceful reaction."

She sighed deeply. "It wasn't supposed to be like this."

"Come back to bed."

She inclined toward the bed for a moment, then shook her head. "I'm confused and upset and I'm really hungry."

So was I, but passion was up there too. I might have convinced her if the faint aroma of cooking food hadn't drifted into the ventilation system. The coffee shop was obviously open.

She fumbled in the pockets of her suit and turned around with a Swiss Army knife in one hand. "I can think of one thing that will help."

"Where did you get that?"

"It's just an arrangement of plastic and metal," she said, as if the answer was obvious. Which, I realized, it was. She grasped the curly hair that fell halfway down her back as if she was going to put it in a ponytail. Christa had sometimes worn it that way.

"What are you doing?"

The blade flashed and then she dropped the ponytail into the trash can. "I need a new look. It's a start."

* * * * *

Sharon looked up from her half-finished short stack with sausage, eggs and milk. "Would you be offended if I told you I've decided you are a bad cook?"

The short, badly cut hair did make a difference. "I told you that Spam wasn't that good."

"It tasted good after liquid food."

The bustle of the coffee shop made me not worry about being overheard. "Why only liquid?"

"Well," she said after she swallowed another forkful of pancakes, "I couldn't eat their food unprocessed."

"Oh. So if one of us were to go there —"

"You'd be on a liquid diet. At least they would know what to offer you. You also wouldn't be able to breathe the air without filtration."

"The Starship Enterprise almost always had compatible atmospheres."

She rolled her eyes. "Your point is?"

"So much for the idea we could just walk off our ship and say, 'Hey, there.' "

"Pallasians can manage with your air, though. Can't eat the food. Water is okay."

"How do you know that?"

"Remember I told you about the explorer?"

I drank the last of my milk. "You mentioned it."

"She could breathe the air, but food nearly killed her. Water saved her life."

"Oh. So she didn't get any pancakes?"

Sharon grinned. Her chipmunk cheeks were adorable. "Not one. Lucky me."

"I'm feeling pretty lucky too." I could tell that every ounce I ate was going right to replenishing my overtaxed body. I would be hungry again in a few hours. Like so many things, it had been ages since being hungry had made me feel alive.

"I can't just eat pancakes and go back to the room with you," she added seriously. "I do have things I must do."

"I believe I offered to help you. Nothing has changed that."

She blotted her mouth with her napkin. I wished my thigh were the napkin. "I wasn't sure. I wanted to be sure."

"Well, it's still really early. I should go back to the hogan and get some things. I'm not prepared for a journey. These clothes are disgusting."

"We'd have been better off if we'd washed them out last night," Sharon said.

"No doubt. I have no regrets."

"Neither do I." Her gaze took away the chill of my damp clothes. "I would love to see the canyon with you. I took very little notice yesterday."

Was it only yesterday? "We could be there and back before checkout time here. I'd be happy for another hot shower after the hike."

She put down her fork and regarded me through half-closed eyes. *:Hiking is not why we're going to need another shower.:*

I felt as if she'd punched the air out of me. The world tipped to one side, and I was dizzy. It was wonderful.

8

"Of course we have canyons," Sharon said. She was starting to sound a little impatient with my endless questions.

I stopped the Jeep at the end of the mud-soaked access road that led to the Spider Rock overlook. "Why of course?"

"Because earth is earth and wind is wind and water is water."

"I'm not a complete idiot," I said snappishly.

"I'm sorry if I sounded patronizing. The forces of nature are universal. They're actually quite simple."

"It takes a universe to explain a blade of grass."
Being along for the ride while she healed herself had
shown me how true that was.

Her smile was slow and warm. "Or a poet. "

"Touché."

"This is one of my favorite vistas," I said. "It'll
only take a few minutes."

We plopped through the mud of the parking lot
onto the nearly dry *de Chelley* sandstone. The
National Park Service had cut steps and added rock
walls with railings to make the short walk easier and
safer.

Spider Rock was a square needle that rose over
eight hundred feet from the canyon floor. It was a
geologist's dream as each successive layer in the pillar
showed how the canyon's sixty-five-million-year-old
beauty had been crafted by sediment from earth's
ancient oceans. Behind the rock, Canyon de Chelley
divided in two, providing a nearly endless vista of deep
reds, swirling orange and the green of a living valley.
The rock stood like a guardian for what had once
been the Navajo people's last refuge.

Sharon drank it in with her usual intensity. "It's
magnificent. All those colors, too, not just the rock
itself, but the red ripples in the canyon walls behind
it. It reminds me of Pallas, in a way. What's the white
stuff on top of Spider Rock?"

I said, seriously, "The bones of disobedient children
that Spider Woman took away in the night."

She gaped at me, then laughed heartily. "That's
priceless. You sounded just like Sela too."

I wasn't sure I liked the comparison. "I'm sure
that every culture in the world — in the universe —

has stories to frighten children into their best behavior."

"Certainly all the ones with children." I opened my mouth to ask the inevitable question, but she shushed me with her fingers on my lips. "Never mind. It's not important."

I couldn't have agreed more. "You shouldn't have touched me." I caught her fingers before they went too far away and kissed them. She wound around me in a breathless coiling of body and mind. Her hands were under my jacket, then under my shirt.

She pushed me against the low wall, and I grabbed for the railing to keep from falling. I clung there, off balance, as her mouth followed her hands. Then she pinned me in place with a demanding kiss while one hand slipped down the front of my jeans.

In a matter of moments my own frantic movements made it clear that I wanted to be out of my clothes. She gave up her delicious assault.

"Thank you for showing me this beautiful place," she whispered in my ear.

"You're welcome," I answered weakly.

I drove the Jeep as far down the muddy access road as I dared, then we hiked the rest of the way. I pointed out unusual formations, the occasional peach tree and the hiding places of prairie dogs. Spring was definitely coming — canyon wrens were already constructing nests.

Sturdy boxes with handholds were my chief method of transporting anything. In less wet weather the Jeep would be just the other side of the wash. Clothing, fortunately, didn't weigh much, so our hike back to the Jeep shouldn't be too awkward.

She let me get what I needed and distribute it between the boxes before she said, "Are you done?" She sounded impatient.

"Just about. Why?"

"I want to finish what I started."

I was wobbly kneed by the time we got back to the Jeep. "You've got to leave me alone for a while or I'll collapse from exhaustion."

Sharon seemed in even more robust health. She looked fantastic in jeans with a warm flannel shirt over a snug T-shirt. She carried the box as if it was empty and at a pace I could hardly keep up with, and I was not out of shape. "It must be time for lunch."

My stomach agreed. "If we stop for food we won't make checkout time. How much cash do you have?" My resources were limited to a small savings account at the local bank. The interest had kept me in food for the last thirteen years.

"Plenty, but all in silver dollars. Easy to replicate, but not very convenient."

"We could change them at the bank." With a relieved sigh, I dropped my box into the back of the Jeep.

Sharon set hers down next to mine. "I think it would be something like a hundred dollars. I spent some yesterday, remember?"

"You came here with just a hundred dollars?

That's hardly the price of a place to sleep for one night."

"It was supposed to be enough for bus fare, maybe some food and a phone call. Once I made it to a city of any size, I would be fine, as long as I didn't need identification." She opened the box she had been carrying and pulled a pouch out of one of the pockets of her suit. She opened it so I could see the glittering, clear stones. "They're collector's grade, and none of them big enough to arouse curiosity."

"Those are diamonds? Where did you — never mind. Compressed carbon is compressed carbon and silver is silver."

She cinched the pouch closed with a grin and slipped it into her hip pocket. "You're learning. Anyway, what I don't need will go to the people I have to see."

I didn't ask about after that. The subject of the future beyond the next few days was too scary. "If we stop at the bank, I can get enough cash for gas and food and you could change your coins into currency. It shouldn't be difficult to find a gem dealer in Flagstaff. Better luck there than Gallup. Gallup is closer, but it's the wrong way."

"It's a plan, then."

I wanted to kiss her. "We're going to the bank and we're getting lunch. I think we'll have to shower and check out of the motel first."

:*I don't claim to know everything, but I've heard of such a thing as paying-by-the-hour. Just in case we forget time.*:

She made forgetting time too easy. It had seemed like a very short time in the hogan, but the sun was approaching zenith. "If we should forget time, remember it's seventy-five miles to Interstate 40, just about two hours given the roads, and then another hour to Holbrook, and if the Jeep lets us, two more hours into Flagstaff. It depends on how ambitious you want to be on the road. At least five hours."

She settled into the passenger seat beside me. "I want to be ambitious about a lot of things, but I don't really care if we make it to Flagstaff today."

I didn't really care if we ever made it at all.

As if she had read my thoughts — and I wasn't sure she hadn't — she said, "But I have to go. There is something I have to do that can't be done by phone."

I backed the Jeep slowly up the access road. "Are you suggesting we get a bright and early start tomorrow?"

"I am trying to cope with the fact that I have no will power where you're concerned."

I crested the access road to the better gravel road along the canyon rim and let the Jeep idle for a minute. She leaned across the seat to quickly kiss me.

"It can be like that the first time." I meant to comfort her.

There were tears in her eyes. "This is not just some sexual obsession."

I took a deep breath. "I don't think you can know that."

"Is that all it is to you?"

"The trouble is, I can't be sure either. This feels a lot like the first time." I was a heartbeat away from turning off the engine and pulling her into my arms.

She was hurt, but I suspected it was because she

knew I was right. "First I was just a face, and now I'm just a body."

"Now you're someone with something you have to do. We don't have to answer all our questions this very moment."

She seemed to relax. "You're right." She giggled. "There's five hours until we get to Flagstaff."

I groaned.

We concluded our pleasure and business at the motel with enthusiasm and a decided lack of urgency, then refilled our hungry stomachs at the coffee shop again. A visit to the grocery store filled the cooler I kept behind the front seat with ice, bottled water and Sharon's now mandatory Coca-Cola. The bank visit took longer than I'd imagined — I had no idea that actually seeing a live person was now so difficult.

When we clambered back into the Jeep, it was late afternoon. I was hungry again. The five hours to Flagstaff seemed like an eternity. Maybe we would stop off in Holbrook, about halfway. Where didn't matter to me since I was already anticipating the bed where we'd spend the night.

We didn't even get out of Chinle. Just after I turned south on 191, I saw flashing red lights in the rearview mirror. "What the hell did I do?" I pulled over.

Sharon clutched my arm. "I don't have any identification."

"You're not driving, it doesn't matter."

:*How am I going to explain it?*:

:I'll figure something out, don't worry.:

The tall, heavyset officer strolled slowly up to my window. "Step out of the car, ma'am."

"What's this about?" I asked, trying not to sound hostile.

"How the hell else am I going to hug you?"

He'd hardly finished speaking when I recognized him. I was out of the Jeep in a flash. "Tommy Ironhorse, you son-of-a-bitch."

:I guess this isn't a problem.: Sharon was definitely curious as to why I was embracing this mountain of a man. Tommy lifted me off my feet and hugged most of the air out of me.

"I heard you were out and about," Tommy said after he put me down. "Then I saw you for myself. Rosa is plenty pissed at you."

I gazed past his dark glasses and saw the laughter in his eyes. "I'm a lousy friend. What can I do?"

"You can fucking come to dinner once every six years. Tonight would be good." He leaned down to peer at Sharon. "And bring your friend. If you don't, Rosa's going to be beat me black-and-blue and then go into labor."

"She's pregnant again? You stud."

Tommy's proud laugh was loud enough to wake the dead. "Like you care."

:I would like to meet your friends, Amy. Please?: Her tone implied that she might not have another chance, which I didn't even want to consider.

Flagstaff would apparently have to wait.

* * * * *

128

We followed Tommy's patrol car to a small house not far from the combined middle and high school. The yard was a mix of dirt and grass, dominated by a profusion of toys and a junglegym. In addition to her own four, Rosa took care of other people's kids when grandparents and aunts had been exhausted.

I'd known Tommy from the first day I'd arrived on the reservation. He'd knocked me down and told me red-haired girls were food for Coyote People. Rosa had made him say sorry and then dragged him away by one ear. He'd been a big, loud bully as a six-year-old, and only Rosa had kept him in line. No one had been surprised when they'd married many years later. Rosa and Tommy were joined in their spirits. They made babies and love and friends the way some people made money. They were the richest people I knew.

Children were jumping up and down, half of them screaming, "Daddy's home!" A short blast of siren from Tommy's car brought Rosa out onto the front porch. When she saw the Jeep she squealed and waddled across the yard as fast as she could. I met her halfway with a heartfelt embrace.

"You worthless bitch," she laughed into my ear. "I'd serve you for dinner, but there's no meat on you as usual."

"I'm sorry, Rosa. It's been too long." Her slight frame seemed too insubstantial to have a cannonball strapped to the front. "When are you due?"

"Two days ago. This one's a kicker." She straightened her back and watched Sharon get out of the Jeep. "Crappy haircut, but you've bagged yourself someone special, I can tell."

"You don't know the half of it," I said. "She dropped into my life right out of the sky."

"Gift from the gods, then. I can believe it." She held out her hand as Sharon drew closer. "Welcome. A friend of Amanda's is always our friend."

"Thank you." Sharon seemed a little shy, but that might have been because of the dervish-possessed children who danced around us.

Tommy kissed Rosa on his way into the house. "I hope there's frybread, woman."

"There will be when you make it," she retorted. She walked with us toward the house with her hands supporting her back. "Actually, there is — I had a massive craving for it."

Dinner was a simple but lengthy affair. Some of the kids disappeared into cars while others were dispatched to the living room with bowls topped by frybread. Rosa would just get them all settled when the first in line wanted more, and someone was always needing another glass of milk.

Tommy did as much as Rosa would let him do. He'd mellowed over the years. He ate his dinner with the youngest on his lap, alternating bites of frybread and chili between his mouth and Paulie's. Anyone who wanted a linear conversation would have been driven insane in under two seconds.

"So, Sharon, how long are you planning to stay? I need the butter." Rosa reached over Tommy as I lifted the dish within her reach.

"No, there's no more bread for you." Tommy bounced the child. "Have some chili. Amanda's place is not exactly a vacation spot."

"It's beautiful," Sharon said. "A bit remote."

A squabble arose from the living room. "Do I have to come in there?" There was silence. Rosa turned to me. "Do you want some more cheese, Amanda?"

"I'm fine, and this is delicious as always," I said. "The hogan is a little rustic, I guess."

"What would you know about my cooking?"

"Rustic, Paulie. She says it's rustic."

"I already said I'm sorry. Does Paulie want some more milk? I'll get it."

"She thinks she can just say she's sorry for not coming to see us for three years." Rosa was talking to Sharon, but she made sure I could hear her as I extracted another gallon of milk from the refrigerator.

"I'll let her answer for that," Sharon said. "The chili really is delicious. I've never had chili before, and I had no idea it tasted so wonderful."

Rosa beamed. "You have a discriminating palate, obviously." She took a deep breath and yelled, "Ned, give your sister her fork back."

"How come when I say it's good I get insults?" I poured the milk. "If I said you make the best frybread I've ever had, you'd ignore me."

Rosa looked pointedly at Sharon, who said with great sincerity, "And your frybread is the best I've ever had."

"It's nice of someone to finally say so," Rosa said sweetly.

"Oh man," I whined to the refrigerator. "It's awfully cold in here."

"It's gonna get colder if you don't start coming around more." Rosa ladled chili into yet another emptied bowl. "That's all for you. And do what I told you. Give your sister her fork back."

"Nothing can be colder than Rosa when she's mad. Take your milk into the other room, Paulie. Don't spill it."

Rosa smacked Tommy with affectionate force. "If I would stay mad I wouldn't be carrying this child nine long months with my back ready to snap in two."

Tommy pulled Rosa onto his lap. "If you stayed mad I'd be to work on time every once in a while."

"Don't mind us," I said.

"As if you care," Rosa said. It had been Rosa who'd driven me to the bus station when I left for college. She'd hugged me and said she hoped I'd find a nice girl and then she'd pushed me up the bus steps. She already knew what I'd hardly told myself. "It's not as if you're one of those vestal virgins."

Sharon blushed at Rosa's meaningful stare. "No, she's certainly not that."

"I never claimed to be." Everyone was picking on me, it seemed. Was I such a bad person?

:They love you. They worried about you.:

I was a bad person. *:I took it for granted. I won't any more.:*

The children were fed and mostly bathed, with Sharon's help, while I washed up the accumulation of dishes. Rosa sat with her feet up, all the while protesting that she could help.

The little ones were in bed, and the older kids settled with a video when Tommy creaked into a kitchen chair. He and Sharon had distinct wet patches from their encounter with Paulie and many bath toys. I carefully arranged the last dish on the loaded drainer. It was a masterpiece of architecture.

"I forgive you," Rosa said. "If you do the dishes every night for a week, I'll forgive you tomorrow, too."

"Sharon and I are heading to L.A. for a short trip, otherwise I would. We were headed for Flagstaff tonight when Tommy pulled me over."

"Typical." Rosa put her feet into Tommy's lap and sighed when he gently rubbed her arches. "You'll have to make it up to me."

"This was a much nicer way to spend an evening." Sharon was looking tired, though.

"You're welcome to bunk here," Tommy said. He blinked at the three pairs of eyes that stared at him. "Whad I say?"

Rosa nudged him with one foot. "They're young and in love."

"Amanda is older than I am," Tommy protested. "Oh! I get it. Motel No-tell."

I threw an ice cube from my soda at him. "I'm four fucking days older than you."

He threw it back. "Watch your language around the kids, shithead."

Rosa looked at Sharon for moral support. "They have been squabbling like this since the moment they met."

"He started it," I said.

"You tried to put some of that red-haired bad medicine on me." The police band radio on the counter squawked. "Damn, I knew it was too good to last." Tommy had an unintelligible conversation with a dispatcher, but it was clear he was needed. "I have to go, darlin'. You radio if you feel anything, and I'll be back here in five minutes."

"I know the drill," Rosa said.

Tommy kissed all of us and dashed away.

"You've tamed him well," I told Rosa.

"Nothing that any other woman with eternal vigilance and the patience of a god couldn't do. I don't want him too tame, though. He wouldn't be my Tommy." She glanced at Sharon and nodded her head in my direction. "You've tamed her pretty well too."

"Like I needed taming," I protested.

"You needed something," Rosa said seriously. "Honestly. You're a shadow."

I didn't know what to say. If I kept eating this way I'd put some weight back where it belonged.

Sharon said quietly, "If you think I've done something good for her, then I am very, very happy."

Rosa stretched her back. "Well, girls, my night-light goes out very early these days."

:Can you do anything for Rosa's back?:

If Sharon was startled, she didn't show it. :I considered it, but I don't think I'd dare touch a pregnant woman. I — I'm not that good.:

Sharon hugged Rosa as if she was made of porcelain. "I hope everything goes wonderfully for the baby."

"It will. I was made to have a dozen."

"The way you and Tommy are going, that might be prophecy." I kissed her good-bye at the door. "I'll be back to see the new baby, I promise."

"Shithead," Rosa said fondly.

"Your friends are nice," Sharon said after we got in the Jeep. "What I had seen of American families wasn't nearly so . . . bonded, I guess."

"Tommy and Rosa have enough love to fill an ocean."

"They reminded me of the Brady Bunch."

I laughed so hard I nearly put us in a ditch. "You did watch too much television."

"Is there anywhere else you can see representations of family life?"

She had a point, but I was still chuckling. "It's a representation, all right, but the Brady Bunch was as alien to me as you aren't."

"There should be more books published on the Internet. I liked reading books when I wasn't studying. But I watched a lot of cable television. Satellites are handy for that. And I have to tell you — the cable channels with all the sex on them? Not one woman has ever had an orgasm the way they do it."

"And I am so grateful you know that."

Sharon grinned. "That's why I let you go first. Just so I could be sure how to do it."

"Ha! Like you let me do anything. Ah was in charge, woman."

She giggled. "Yeah, and Tommy thinks he's in charge, too."

"That's cold. What is this, insult Amanda night?"

"I'll make it up to you." She lifted my hand from the gearshift and put it on her thigh.

I had to take it back to turn into a drive-through. "I want a shake, how about you?" My hand was lonely.

"Sure — wait, one of those sundaes. Chocolate."

I ordered and pulled forward. "Rosa's chili is divine, but my stomach is less fond of it."

Sharon put a hand on her stomach. "Is this heartburn? Something else that doesn't feel remotely like I thought it would."

When we got back to the motel she seemed

troubled by more than heartburn, but when I asked, she kissed me and absolutely forced me to kiss her back.

We were finally in Flagstaff shortly after lunchtime. Sharon continued to rise with the sun, and our good mornings had been extremely satisfactory. Sharon was hoarse from answering my questions, but she was patient so I kept asking. Pallas was not a perfect world, but they managed to feed, clothe and educate everyone. No one fell through the cracks. She let me hear some of her memories of words and singing — it reminded me of whale song, but that's not really a close comparison. It was dissonant and harmonic, sometimes percussive but always evocative in the way that Sela's song had made me think of a summer day.

The Flagstaff yellow pages turned up a gemstone dealer and though it wasn't top dollar, Sharon sold four of the little twinkling stones for fifty twenty-dollar bills.

"He didn't even ask me where I got them." She gave me half of the cash. "Just in case."

"I don't need it."

"Consider it safekeeping then. For emergencies."

We left the beautiful mountain town with a full tank of gas. The farther west we went the lower the elevation and the more desolate the terrain became. We refilled at the last gas station before the Tehachapi Pass and, after driving for what seemed like hours without moving, we arrived in Barstow long after sundown. My butt was asleep, and I couldn't face another greasy burger.

All along the highway in Barstow were motels with no vacancies. I pulled into the first one we came to that wasn't full and that had a coffee shop nearby. As far as food went, I'd picked well — the vegetables were even fresh, not canned. During the day Sharon had graduated from beef to poultry and was now investigating seafood.

Exhausted from the inactivity of sitting, I proposed a short walk before we went to bed. I was so stiff and sore that I was actually thinking about sleep.

The walk did us both good. We were almost back to the motel when some yahoo in a passing truck yelled, "I'm hung like a horse, pretty mama, come and get it!"

"Please," I muttered.

Sharon was laughing. "Did he really think that would entice us to have sex with him?"

"In his dreams." We walked past the motel lobby toward our room. A short-skirted woman in a very tight blouse came out from one room, still counting the bills in her hand. "On the other hand . . ." I glanced up at the sign. "Maybe he thought we were in the market." I had registered us at a motel that advertised it had adult movies in all the rooms.

When Sharon saw the leopard-skin print that covered everything from the bed to the walls to the toilet lid, she had a fit of the giggles. "It's like something off the Playboy Channel."

Through the thin walls the sound of coital bliss was all too unmistakable. "We're not going to be able to sleep," I complained. "And what do you know about the Playboy Channel?"

"Cable television, remember? Let's make our own noise." Sharon shimmied out of her clothes and plopped on the bed. It undulated.

"Oh jeez, a waterbed." I'd never slept on one in my life.

"This is great." She stretched out and closed her eyes. "It's just like home ... just like home."

I brushed my teeth and examined my face in the mirror. The haunted look was gone and my cheeks were less hollow. I needed to do something about my hair as much as Sharon did. Maybe in the morning we could take an hour to get haircuts.

I snuggled up to Sharon, then realized she was asleep. So much for the power of leopard-skin prints. I pulled the blankets over us and closed my eyes.

The banging of the headboard on the other side of the wall kept me up for a while, then it stopped. I was quickly asleep, and I dreamed of a coral ocean with green fronds swaying in the tide.

The outskirts of San Bernardino greeted us with malls and numerous places to get our hair cut. Sharon didn't want to take the time, but she had to agree she looked a little wild. She did not want to inspire distrust when she finally met the women she was looking for.

In less than an hour, my hair looked more like I remembered it — shiny instead of dingy, thanks to protein revitalizing mousse spritz freeze, or something like that. I just nodded. Once the stylist recovered from her horror at the condition my hair was in, she managed to clip and shape it out of my eyes and trim it so it just brushed my shoulders.

I waited at the front of the salon with some trepidation. While I was getting my hair washed, Sharon had sent me a thought. *:I hope blondes have more fun.:*

When she emerged from the cutting frenzy she had been transformed from dark-blonde-brown to gold with platinum highlights. It took me a moment to adjust. It would be even harder for someone to recognize her now. It would take someone like me, who had stared at her picture over and over, to see that the resemblance was still there.

"Well, am I a bombshell?"

I laughed. "Not hardly. You're too small to be a bombshell." I mimed a quick squeezing motion with my hands and arched my eyebrows suggestively. "I think there's plenty of you already, though."

"I could get a Wonderbra." Sharon looked down her front.

"A wonder what?"

Sharon snickered. "What planet have you been on?"

I had to laugh. She knew more about modern life than I did. "You don't need to gloat."

"I'm absolutely certain that if I told you a joke about a President, a cigar and an intern, you wouldn't know what the heck I was talking about."

"I don't think I want to know."

She was grinning. "You're better off. I'm hungry again — how about an Egg McMuffin?"

As we walked toward the Jeep, I said, "Your arteries are going to be very American in no time."

"If you would rather buy a stove and whip up something more wholesome, I'm all for it. It's going to take longer, though. It's called *fast* food for a reason."

"I'm just pointing out the dangers of the all-McDonald's diet." I struggled with the Jeep's anti-quated seat belt.

"We'll have broccoli and tofu for dinner."

"There's no need to be mean. I'm just trying to help."

I managed to find the freeway on-ramp. After that it got messy. Sharon had the map and advised me the shortest route was to continue until we got to 605, then take 10 west to 710 south then exit to 60 west and look for 110 north to South Flower.

We got lost. It didn't help that everyone drove with a cutthroat insistence on gaining the best lane position, and everyone had their own definition of what that was. If I drove more slowly so as not to misread signs, people honked and swerved around me. If I tried to speed up there was always someone cutting me off. I missed the exit to 60 west, and by the time we found it we were most of the way into the downtown area anyway.

I had worked myself up into a good lather. Every other driver was a son-of-a-bitch bastard from a tribe with no name.

"I think this is it," Sharon said. She had wisely kept quiet the past twenty miles. She pointed and I swerved over two lanes, heedless of the honking protests, and pulled into a parking lot. I was getting the hang of driving in L.A.

"This is it?" I couldn't imagine what business Sharon could possibly have at the *National Weekly Star*. It was the kind of so-called newspaper than ran headlines like "Teen has Bigfoot Baby."

"This is where I find somebody." She slipped out of the Jeep before I could ask any more questions.

She'd told me very little about what she had to do. She'd promised she would tell me more after she'd done it. It was just a message that needed to be delivered, one that would help the women who had helped the lost explorer.

She was back in just a few minutes. "That was frustrating. They'd only give her a message. I couldn't see her."

"So what do we do?"

"We wait. There's nothing else to do."

I looked longingly at the store that took up the bottom floor of the building next door. We were out of ice and cold drinks and, after coping with the most horrendous traffic I'd ever experienced, I was in need of food and caffeine. What passed for air was threatening to make me wheeze. The only blue was painted on a noisy bus that clanked by. I'd already decided the sky was high-country mud.

I was just about to suggest to Sharon that we find something to eat and come back when a small-framed, fast-moving, dark-haired woman came out of the building and glanced around.

"That's her," Sharon breathed. She got out of the Jeep.

No way was I going to let her do this alone.

She saw us moving toward her and stopped so we had to come to her. Her dark hair and olive skin made me think she might have some native blood.

"Did you leave this message?" She held out a piece of paper, and she looked really pissed off.

"I did," Sharon said. "I want to talk to you about Sirena."

"Who the fuck are you?"

"Sirena's messenger."

The woman exhaled as if Sharon had slugged her. "You have some sort of proof, I hope."

"Yes. We need some privacy. And I need to talk to your daughter."

"Nobody talks to my daughter." The woman stepped backward as if she was going to run.

Sharon reached out slowly. "Let me prove that I can."

The woman's jaw went slack as Sharon took her hand. When Sharon let go she took a shaky breath. "I'll take you to see her. Let me get my things." She practically ran back into the building.

"Who was that?" I was more confused than when we had arrived. "Who's Sirena?"

"Sirena is the name they gave the lost explorer. Just like I gave Sela her name. Our mouths won't form the real sounds."

I was neck-deep in alien land again. It wasn't getting any easier to believe or understand. "So who was that? And who is her daughter?"

"That was Tamar Reese, and her daughter is also Sirena's daughter."

I closed my eyes. "Of course. I should have known. Aliens, babies, the *National Weekly Star*. Makes perfect sense."

Tamar came out of the building with a man. She seemed to be trying to get rid of him. Her words barely reached us in the heavy air. "I'll see you tomorrow, then."

He followed Tamar, glancing curiously at us.

"This isn't good," Sharon whispered. "This is not good."

"Come on, Tamar," he said. "I always know when you've got something good. What is it, more of your alien-lesbian connection? You can tell me."

"They're just friends, really." Tamar was walking even faster. Sharon started to back away, pulling me with her.

He was not dissuaded. He studied both of us as we backed away. He fixed on Sharon's face. "One of your friends looks familiar."

"This doesn't concern you," Tamar snapped. "You might know more about swamp gas and conspiracy theories than just about any person on the planet, but I still don't know why they tolerate your arrogance. Would you get lost?"

He shrugged, obviously used to being unwanted. "What can I say? Now I'm really curious." He spoke directly to Sharon. "I know you from somewhere. You weren't a blonde, though."

"Get. Lost. Now." Tamar turned her back on him and stalked toward the back of the parking lot. We followed her.

There was silence for a moment, then he called, "You were in a NASA uniform. I saw you when I worked for the *Post*."

Sharon muttered, "This isn't good."

His footsteps were loud behind us.

Tamar said, "What the hell is this about? Who are you, really?"

He broke into a run. I whirled around to face him. Growing up with Tommy Ironhorse had taught me a thing or two. "Back off!"

He stopped short. "I don't know who you are, I don't care. But I am back in legitimate news when I tell the world that Christa McAuliffe is alive."

Sharon gasped, and he looked triumphant. "The hair almost fooled me, but I covered every press conference you did at the Cape."

Tamar was glancing back and forth between me, Sharon and the man, as if trying to discern who was telling the truth. She finally set her sights on Sharon. "You want to take it from the top? Just who are you?"

There was a flash of silver light and a sound like an avalanche or an earthquake. I'd heard it before.

The world around me melted like watercolors in the rain.

:Aaaaammmmmyyyy, tttaaakkkeee mmmyyy hhaaaaaaand.:

I turned without awareness of my body. Sharon was swimming toward me, rippling around brilliant threads of silver. I took the hand she held out and she yanked us both into one of the shimmering strands.

Part 3:
The Dawning

9

We were sitting in the Jeep. I was saying something and Sharon answered, "This is where I find somebody." She started to get out of the Jeep, but I clamped my hand on her arm.

"What the hell just happened?"

She turned back, looking frightened and guilty. "I had to do something or he was going to be a very big problem."

I remembered the man with Tamar, but Sharon hadn't even gone inside yet. *:What the hell just happened?:*

"I jumped us back. Just a few minutes."

"What do you mean, just a few minutes?" I was distracted by the clanking of a bus painted bright blue. "I saw that bus before."

"Yes, you did."

"You're scaring me," I whispered. I had thought being afraid was behind me.

"You never asked how we travel. I didn't think you wanted to know."

"I just want to know what happened to that guy. To Tamar?"

"Space isn't the ultimate mystery, time is."

"Don't go fucking Zen on me. What are you saying?"

"Time can be the longest distance between two places. It can also be the shortest."

My head started to pound. "Are you trying to say you use time travel?"

"No, we use time to travel."

"What the fuck is the difference?"

Sharon put her head in her hands. "The difference has occupied learned scholars for centuries. I doubt I'd be any good at explaining it."

"That's convenient."

"It's the truth. If I thought I could have made him forget seeing me without Tamar freaking out, I would have done it. But we both know I'm not very good at that."

"Then what exactly did you do?" An implausible hope started to beat inside me.

"I took us into time, along the thread we were in.

I didn't even know I could until I first got here and you broke your leg."

"When I what?" I realized I was shouting. "One of these days you're going unzip your neck and I'll find out I've been screwing a giant lizard!" I was getting that panicky feeling again, like I didn't know what she was anymore.

"This isn't helping," Sharon snapped.

"I didn't break my leg."

"You just don't remember me pulling you through the thread. It was one of the few things I did perfectly."

Through gritted teeth I said, "Talk very slowly."

"You broke your leg when you tried to help me. I healed it. I did too good a job. Something about a scar going away. You got out of the bathtub, and you were hostile and suspicious, and I had just looked at the books on your shelf. I mean, I was thrilled to actually touch a book. And I pull it off the shelf and there it is, the accident, the reason I exist. I knew you'd recognize me, and you were already half freaked out about being healed. I panicked."

She kicked at a wrinkle in the floor mat. "I thought — I was wrong — that I could just fix every-thing by starting over and making sure you didn't break your leg. I'd make sure you didn't recognize me. Sela had a conniption."

"But I recognized you anyway." Of all the things that didn't make sense, this was top of the list.

Sharon stared at me, exasperated. "How was I supposed to know you could tap into my thoughts? I go to sleep and the next thing I know you recognize me and you're trying to choke me to death!"

"It seems to me it was the other way around. You're the one who forced me to remember all of it, just because you were curious!" What had I been thinking for the last three days? That Sharon and I would live happily ever after? What a fool I was.

"Haven't I already said I was sorry?"

It wasn't enough. "This was a pretty big secret."

"It's just the way we can travel. Time intersects with space in specific ways. Travel a time thread, switch when you need to — you can go anywhere and step out again as long as you emerge at the same universal time. The better you are at it, the farther you go with less elapsed universal time."

"Can you go to any point in the past or future?" I had to ask. I had told myself for thirteen years that I would give anything to undo sending that fax. I would give anything to have the life I would have had back.

"The future threads don't exist yet." She said it as if she was telling a child it couldn't have a cookie that wasn't made yet. "You can go to a point in the past, you can look around, but you're not really there. you're just looking into the thread."

"But we're here. Six, maybe seven minutes to live over again."

"The universe has its own time. It has nothing to do with clocks and calendars. Time passes and creates windows and rivers. We can make a tiny step back because it hasn't drifted yet."

"But what about what was meant to be? Tamar should have met you by now." I was so confused I had a tight, white hot headache right between my eyes.

"Meant to be by whom? You get all your notions

from television and wonder why I can't explain the way things really are?" Her exasperation was plain. "Time is not like a videotape you can rewind and see exactly the same way again. The threads are much more fluid. They come apart and rejoin in different ways, and that has no effect on the future because universal time never starts over."

"But that man hasn't recognized you in this future."

"I took the chance that if we did go back, just a bit, we could step out again. And we could. Here we are."

"And if it hadn't worked?"

"I'd have put us back and we'd have tried something else."

"What happened to the Tamar on the thread where we were?"

She blinked. "I don't understand. Tamar is in the building."

My head hurt so much I wanted to cry. "No, she was standing right over there. What happened to that Tamar?"

"There's only one Tamar."

"This isn't right," I stammered. "Don't the moral implications bother you at all? What if people did this for personal gain? To make sure their enemies were never born?"

"It doesn't work that way."

"But you just did it." I couldn't hold the tears back any longer. "My head feels like it's going to explode."

"Amy," she said softly. Her hand on my forehead was heavenly. "I should have thought of this — it's just from the temporal readjustment. It's another reason not to go to any time but where you belong."

Past is future, future is past, grandmothers being their own granddaughters — it was the fodder of countless books and movies. It gave me a blinding headache.

I loved the feel of Sharon's arms around me, and the way her heartbeat sounded in my ear. But my mind was swirling with one thought: I could go back to my past.

My life had veered downward the moment liquid oxygen and hydrogen were ignited and seven people died. I was so thrilled at being alive and in her arms that I'd almost forgotten about them.

She made me want to forget. My friends wanted me to forget. I wanted to forget. Now more than ever before, I knew that I couldn't. I shouldn't. My past had brought me here and I wanted to be here. If I'd been the only one who'd paid a price, it would be different. But it hadn't been just me. Not hardly me at all. Those seven people and their children and parents had paid, and the coin they'd paid with was too precious for me to accept.

Sharon said I couldn't change anything, but I had to try. How could I accept the future when I now knew so clearly that it existed because of the horrible thing I'd done in my past? How could I accept happiness at such a price?

She let go of me when I pushed her gently away and huddled against the door of the Jeep, dispirited because she could not make me understand how time worked and uncertain — though she tried to hide it — that I didn't know more about it than she did. She already knew that she had not been told everything about her abilities and that the science she counted on was not infallible.

"I don't know what you expect me to do," she said finally.

"I don't know what I expect either. I made a mistake and you're alive because of it. And seven people aren't." It sounded brutal, put that way, but it was the only way to say it.

"I didn't get born on purpose. You didn't make a mistake so you could sleep with me later." She straightened suddenly. "There she is. We're back on track."

I looked out the rear window. Tamar was alone and walking in our direction. Sharon got out of the Jeep.

What did Sharon mean, back on track? Was Tamar fated to walk out of the building to meet us after all? Was there any way of knowing what was fate and what was luck and what was a mystery not meant for comprehension?

I got out of the Jeep too and stood watching while Sharon waited. When Tamar looked her way curiously as she passed, Sharon said, "I have a message from Sirena."

Tamar stopped in her tracks. "Who the fuck are you?"

"Someone with a message for you and your daughter from Sirena."

Tamar started to back away. "No way are you talking to my daughter. If you bother me again, I'll call the cops."

Sharon put her hands behind her back. It made her look so harmless. "I can prove what I'm saying, if you'll give me a chance. You didn't want to believe Maddy, but you listened."

I had no idea who Maddy was, but now was not the time to find out.

Tamar went still. She stared at Sharon for a very long minute, her intense eyes never letting up. "Where do you know Maddy from?"

"My home. She wants you to know she made it. So did Sirena. That's the message for you and the others. I have a different one for your daughter, and it's important that she get it."

Tamar moved toward Sharon so quickly, I stepped between them. She looked me up and down. "And what are you?"

"A crazy woman who's been living in a canyon for thirteen years." I didn't say "Don't fuck with me," but the words hung in the air anyway.

"I'll just bet. Let me guess — you talk to spirit guides, make powerful medicine."

She did have some native blood. It was in the shape of her eyes and her high cheekbones. "She's the one who makes the medicine. I was minding my own business on the rez until she showed up."

"Which rez?" She asked with the assurance that I would fail her test.

"Navajo. I grew up with Dineh." I used the Navajo word for themselves — it simply meant "the people" — to see if she knew what it meant.

"I'm Dineh from my grandmother, who was Born for Water." She said it with the clear expectation that

I could not possibly produce credentials that matched, not with my white skin and red hair.

Sharon had credentials. She held out the hand that bore Edna Beaker's ring. "I have made a great friend with Born for Water."

Tamar examined the ring with a shaky breath. Sharon's hand waved around a little, and Tamar grasped it to look more steadily.

:*I am Sirena's messenger. I can talk to your daughter.:*

Tamar reeled, and I caught her before she fell.

I half carried Tamar to the nearest place we could sit down, a coffee bar with a few post-lunch stragglers. Her color came back with a few sips of water, and the cashier ignored us once Sharon purchased mocha-somethingaccino for all of us.

Three healthy swallows of real coffee made me feel like a new woman.

"Believe me, I'm not a fainter," Tamar said. "You have no idea how I wondered if anyone would come and if we'd ever know — but they're safe, they made it home."

Sharon nodded. "We had the ability to give them back what they left behind — almost as good as new."

She was being cryptic on my account. "Should I leave?"

Tamar looked as if she thought it was a good idea.

Sharon put her hand on my knee. "Stay. Like I promised, I'll tell you all about it later."

"You don't look like her," Tamar said.

"I'm . . ." Sharon was struggling for the right words. "I'm just a messenger. I'm not Pallasian, but I'm from there."

"I don't understand," Tamar said, "but I don't have to. I've learned to take quite a bit on faith."

"When can I see her?"

"How did you know you needed to?" Tamar drained the last of her coffee — she'd made short work of it.

"Amazing what you can read on the Internet. Sirena remembered your affiliation with that paper, and they keep an eye on it. You've actually told quite a bit about what's happened since she left."

"I hoped — you don't know how I hoped that would be the case. I'm going to stop working there soon, and I took a chance with the picture."

What picture I had no idea. No one was going to explain anything to me.

Sharon was saying, "That's why I finally came. Alien love child — cute."

Tamar was grinning with relief. "I was hoping somehow I would be told what I needed to know. Gallina is not in dire straits, but she soon could be. If I didn't get help from you, I'd have to try conventional means. That's risky, for obvious reasons."

Obvious, right. They might as well have been talking in Japanese for all I understood.

"Sirena knows she's still in big trouble for having done it, but what's done is done, and there was responsibility to be taken. So here I am."

"Holy mother of God, here you are." Tamar's gaze flicked to me. "She's okay, right?"

I slurped the last of my coffee and tried to look stupid.

Sharon's lips twitched. "Yes. She's okay."

"Let's go, then." Tamar was on her feet, ready to move at what I perceived was her usual energetic pace.

They decided, without asking me, that it would be better if I followed with the Jeep. Sharon got in Tamar's sleek minivan while Tamar went back inside to let someone know where she was. When she came back the man who'd recognized Sharon was with her, but since we were both hidden in vehicles, he accepted Tamar's good-byes and walked down the street. Was everything the way it would have been before?

Before what, I asked myself. Was he supposed to recognize Sharon and put an end to whatever she was doing here? Or was that the accident? Had Sharon put things right by eluding him the second time around?

I was by myself for the first time in four days. I had plenty to think about paradoxes and fixing the past, but it gave me such a headache I just couldn't cope. Besides, it was all I could do to keep up with Tamar.

Tamar drove like a wild woman. The Jeep didn't have the power steering she obviously relied on to complete dangerous maneuvers that put us on the right off-ramps and on-ramps as we wound our way north. Everyone drove like that. I fully expected an accident at least once a mile, but it never happened. We just barreled along the 110, the 5, the 10, the 605, the 210 and so on, cloverleafing on and off freeways and boulevards until I was nauseated.

My nausea finally calmed down when we got off of

210 onto the kind of two-lane highway I was used to. San Gabriel Canyon Road was cooler, too, with more trees and the hint of moisture I preferred in the air. Tamar drove a little more sedately, then surprised me by turning quickly into a driveway that was blocked by a gate. She had a brief conversation with the gate-keeper, who then gave me a narrow, not particularly friendly stare as I passed through the gate behind Tamar. A small marker, hardly visible from the road, read, "Gardens Campus."

We wound through the trees into a side canyon, passing what looked like bungalows and classrooms, then an auditorium and a sports field. Except for teh small marker there had been no sign at the gate, but we were obviously on some sort of college grounds.

We parked in front of a building that looked like it might be apartments — lots of windows with curtains and blinds.

Tamar was waiting for me impatiently. "You don't have to lock your car here."

Whatever, I thought. I made a point of locking the door. She got on my nerves. We went inside to cool, moist air. The bottom floor had a large common room with grade-school-age kids having a lesson of some sort. Beyond that there appeared to be a cafeteria. My stomach growled.

Tamar led us in the opposite direction to a set of double doors. I knew what the muffled pandemonium was before she opened the door. Toddlers, and lots of them.

I immediately knew which one was Tamar's daughter. Her stillness set her apart as much as her long, nearly white hair. She looked up the moment

Tamar entered and ran quickly through the toddler frenzy to be picked up and kissed. She never said a word or made a sound.

Tamar led us to a small playroom that was empty, and the child immediately went to a table her size and began arranging blocks. Tamar and I settled uncomfortably on the low chairs, but Sharon opted to kneel on the carpet next to the little girl.

"Gallina, these women have come a long way to see you."

Gallina looked up, obviously understanding.

Tamar said, "I can tell she's accepted you. I don't think you'll frighten her."

"How can you tell?" Sharon picked up a block and put it on top of the structure Gallina had started.

"I used to think it was maternal instinct. But when she didn't develop speech and I knew so vividly what she wanted — well, I suspected she was developing the part of her that came from Sirena."

This little girl was a telepath? I didn't know what to think, but then I had the odd idea that the three red blocks in front of me should be on the other side of the table. I handed them to Gallina, who smiled and went back to building.

"See what I mean?" Tamar shrugged. "It's so subtle I didn't even think it was there. But now I do. The doctors say that there's no reason she shouldn't be talking. Her vocal cords are there and she does yell sometimes if she gets seriously hurt. But no attempt at words."

"I think I can fix that," Sharon said softly. "I learned her way first — talking came much later. A few days ago, in fact."

Tamar was clearly puzzled, but it made sense to me. Sharon's voice had been quite hoarse at first. I'd put it down to a cold, but disuse was just as likely.

Gallina had stopped playing. She looked at Sharon with confusion, then slid onto the carpet next to her. She shook her head.

"The trouble is, she's good at getting her message across," Sharon said. "She doesn't see any reason to do anything differently when she gets what she wants this way."

"She's surrounded by people willing to work hard to hear her. The world isn't like that. It won't be like that." Tamar fidgeted. She was obviously unused to sitting for any length of time. "There are all the ethical considerations — she has to understand that she's special and there are obligations that go with that."

"She's how old? Five? Six?" I was not that good at judging age, but a five-year-old understanding obligations was not exactly what I considered possible.

"She'll be three at the end of May. Her development and growth seems to be a little accelerated. Sirena's contribution again, probably."

Sharon was stretching out on the carpet, and Gallina joined her. They both put their feet in the air. "I'm going to be a while," Sharon said. "I'm showing her the way to teachers."

"Teachers where Sirena is?" Tamar was unsettled by this development, but I could sense her relief as well.

"Yes," Sharon said. "There's no one here to teach her. When she's a little older she'll be able to link you in and you can find out more about what she's learning."

"I'm hoping she . . . she's still young. I just have high hopes, that's all." Tamar turned to me. "Would you like me to show you around? This is a long way from the rez, but we've kept some of the concepts."

I let Tamar pull me away from Sharon. "This is yours? This college?"

"It's part college and part grade school and everything in between. Women who have been . . . touched by the same experience come here to share it, and some bring their children in hopes that they'll learn to be better people. It's what we all hope for."

She showed me through the common room and cafeteria to a garden entrance. Squash and tomatoes grew in profusion, with rows of grapes and orange trees. Huge solar panels shaded the less hardy plants, and the entire area was roofed by fine mesh to keep out birds and larger insects. It was an astonishing undertaking in the middle of a sprawling major metropolitan area.

"I come here because the air feels like home." Tamar was inhaling deeply as we walked.

"I feel it." The air was full of life.

"I used to be a reporter in the Four Corners area. My mother passed for white and moved us to Kansas City, but as soon as I was old enough I was back near the rez."

Two women carrying pruning equipment greeted Tamar as she walked slowly down a row of carrots. I guessed they were lesbians, but it was hard to tell when everyone was wearing flannel and Birkenstocks.

:She's cute.:

I glanced over my shoulder and caught both of them looking me over.

:Thank you.: What else was there to say? Tamar certainly had an interesting bunch of women here. Very interesting indeed.

The two women gaped and laughed, then hurried away.

What had Tamar called it? A place where women touched by the same experience could gather? Gather for what, I wondered. "What are you doing here? What's your goal?"

For the first time since I'd seen her, Tamar seemed completely calm inside. "To be ready."

When she said nothing more, I had to ask. "For what?"

"The future isn't what it used to be. We are at the dawning of a new age of reality, though most people don't know it. The others will come." Her mouth twisted bitterly for a moment. "Some of them, not Sirena's people, are already here. They're not what I'd call nice. When all the others make themselves known, there is going to be a choice of who we as a single people will choose to walk beside us into the new dawn. Our goal here is to be ready to choose. Hesitation will be fatal. It's the only act of free will that will matter to our world for the next thousand years. Choosing well."

Not even a week ago I would have heard Looney Tunes music and looked for the nearest exit. Today I knew that Tamar believed she was telling the truth.

I had no reason not to believe her, either, not after all I'd experienced through contact with Sharon. I had been remade in just a few days. I had found a remnant of self-worth amidst all my mistakes. I had discovered there was a chance I could change what I had done. I still couldn't puzzle through what would happen if I was successful. Would I still be standing here, listening to Tamar's vision of the future? Would I wake up with Sharon's arms around me?

How could I know? All I did know was that it was my mistake to fix. If I didn't try, I didn't deserve this future.

10

Our stay stretched from a few hours to a few days. Sharon and Gallina were inseparable. I bided my time — this is what Sharon had come here to do. When it was done I had my own demands.

I watched the clouds move over this canyon. It was both full of life and motion and surrounded with stillness. I didn't see space shuttles and dying craft in the weather, but I used the time to think.

I couldn't think my way through Sharon's time paradox. I told myself wryly that there was a reason it was called a paradox. Sharon's position was that the future would happen anyway because the universe has its own time. Moving back a few minutes for convenience meant nothing to the universe. Going back further had no guarantee of success because once the universe considered something done, it had no need to keep the past tidy. But I had a need to tidy up the past — it was more than a matter of convenience to me.

Besides, I wasn't buying it. Granted she had managed to get here, and granted the people who created her had some technology working for them. Maybe I couldn't comprehend their version of time because I just wasn't evolved enough. Maybe I couldn't figure it out because I wanted it to work my way. The way that let starship captains go back in time to save the planet and change the past and secure the future.

I listened to the teachers and I felt the harmonious bonds that tied this place together. At first I thought they were the back-to-nature, clean-living type of group. There were certainly enough organic baby greens and fat-, wheat-, dairy-, sugar- and salt-free menu items. But the depths here were deeper than communal living arrangements. Many of the students and children didn't even live on the premises. They were bound by a common belief that a profound change was coming and that they had been lucky enough to get tipped off in time to prepare.

I had been suspicious of religious fanaticism, but the chapel was multidenominational. Nothing anyone learned here was supposed to supplant their own beliefs, only illuminate and strengthen them. In a single day, I saw endless acts of what my grandmother would have called Christian kindness, and yet women competed aggressively on the soccer field and I'd heard more than a few heated arguments. There was just no undercurrent of win-at-all-costs viciousness that seemed to permeate the rest of the world.

At times I overheard someone saying that a matter would need Tamar's viewpoint. It was clear she was the driving force behind Gardens Campus. I still remembered how the women's support group at Princeton would get bogged down for weeks trying to decide on a color for a poster that was woman-positive and didn't carry patriarchal overtones. Events would go without publicity because the proponents of orange had called the green-lovers capitalists of the worst kind. In retrospect, I thought it was because there wasn't enough power to go around and everyone was picking at the one piece of pie. Very little ever got done.

That was not a problem here. Things got done because people had jobs to do and they were decidedly businesslike about the work of running this place. One of the accountants had a sign over her desk: Even dreams have payroll taxes.

Tamar was unmistakably in charge, but any power trip that might have resulted was balanced by J. T., the other founder. She was away on personal business, but I couldn't wait to meet her. If Tamar was the iron will behind this place, J. T. was the heart.

I watched the clouds and I thought about what I'd never done — contributed to something larger than my own misery.

* * * * *

A few days became a week. Sharon and I had been given a guest room, but she was rarely in it except to sleep. I missed her warmth. I certainly missed the sex. The room to think and breathe for a while was welcome, and I was living in what was practically a lesbian utopia. I was still lonely, though, lonely for her. It didn't help that I had the feeling that Sharon was avoiding me. If I was right, I also knew the reason why.

I went looking for her almost a week to the hour we had arrived. I found her in the gymnasium pool, teaching Gallina to swim. It didn't look like Gallina needed much help. She and Sharon were like fish in the water. Just frolicking about, they completed stunts that would have made synchronized swimmers green with envy.

They finally climbed the pool steps, laughing and squeezing the water out of their hair.

Gallina waved at me. "Come have fun, Amy!"

"Maybe later," I called. There was no question but that Sharon had been good for Gallina. She talked now, whole sentences. The words had been there all along. She just hadn't seen the need before and, child-like, had assumed that what was easier for her must be the right way to go through life.

Sharon dripped her way to the bench beside me. "It's time for her lesson with Sela. I'm free tonight, all night. I miss you."

She caressed me with her thoughts, and I said sternly, "Stop that. You'll give Gallina ideas."

"Spoilsport."

"Sharon, we have to talk. You know we have to talk."

She looked guilty. I was right, she had been avoiding me. "I know. There's a lot I have to say."

"A lot you have to hear."

She nodded. "Tamar says that Gallina will start regular school next week. It's time for me to get out of the way. I'm not her mother."

"Are you going home?" It was the question I had dreaded asking because I knew the answer.

"I don't want to."

"But you have to."

"I want to talk about this tonight, okay? I promise I'll be in the room after dinner." Her lower lip quivered. I wanted to kiss her. She wanted me to kiss her. But I didn't.

"Thanks," she said.

"For what?"

"For at least wanting to." She walked away, leaving damp footprints on the cement. They dried quickly, leaving no sign that she had ever been there.

Tamar waylaid me as I was carrying my dinner tray to one of the communal tables. "I'd like to talk to you, if that's okay."

She'd virtually ignored me for the past week. She must need something that only I could provide. "Sure." This ought to be interesting, I thought.

She led me to a table where her own dinner — as healthy and wholesome as my own — waited. I was missing McDonald's.

Her opening statement was typical of her. "You don't like me, do you?"

"I don't have a reason to like you." She brought out brutal honesty in me.

"I don't like you either, so there's hope that we can be honest with each other about everything else as well."

I had to go along with that way of thinking. "You must have a point."

"I do. We need a lawyer, one who believes."

"I'm not a lawyer."

"But you could be one in two short years. At least that's what Sharon thinks."

"No way — I have thirteen-odd years of case history to catch up on. No J.D. program would accept my master's work without an update."

"Okay, three years."

"In three years an asteroid could demolish the planet."

"In three years you'll be three years older than you are now."

"Why do you need a lawyer?"

Tamar smiled slightly. She thought she'd hooked me. "We want to expand, maybe build another site, get some zoning laws changed, trademark some of our work, gain accreditation for our medical program —"

"Why don't you have a lawyer now?"

"Ever heard a lawyer joke?"

"Yeah. The oldest one I know was by John Adams."

"We didn't think we needed that kind of energy."

"And you dislike me enough to think I have it?" In a strange way, I felt complimented.

"No, I dislike you enough to know you'll be honest and tell me when we — J. T. and me — make mistakes."

"You've already made them."

She didn't like hearing it. With her cheeks sucked in she said tightly, "Such as?"

"This is a great location. A nice hideaway. You're already too big for it, and you've got no place to grow. You're thinking of a spin-off and place where you can shift a few things to give everyone some more breathing room. Wrong idea." My jumbled thoughts of the last week cemented in my mind. "You should be thinking about replication, not satellites. If your magic is going to work, there can't be a mother house. Everyone has to have equal access, and you have to get out in the real world and touch ordinary people. You can only go as far as the most ordinary person among you can go. If you and J. T. get too far ahead, the rubber band will snap."

She looked at me for a long time. I watched anger, resignation, frustration, superiority and a good dose of dislike for me and my attitude flow over her face. She swallowed hard. "We need a lawyer."

"I'm not a lawyer."

Through stiff lips, she muttered, "I'm trying to ask you to stay."

I knew that had to be a hard admission for her. She was utterly independent. "Are you asking because if I stay, Sharon will too?"

"Sharon can't stay."

Her flat acceptance disheartened me more than I wanted to show. "I can't stay either. I have family and friends who have stood by me when I've given nothing in return."

"They're obviously saints." She half smiled. "That, or they understand the definition of family and friendship better than you do."

I wanted to snap back, except that she was right. I looked at my cold dinner. Broccoli and tofu — it made me want Spam, just a little. "I won't say that I'll never come back." I couldn't begin to explain to Tamar that I had to fix something that happened thirteen years ago and if this place was still around after that I might show up. I couldn't explain it to myself.

"That's something. I was going to have you meet J. T. — she's back from her family business."

"I'd still like to meet her."

"I'll take you over to her office as soon as we're done."

After we ate our dinner in near silence, Tamar escorted me to a small office where a woman about my age was leafing through paperwork with a discouraged air. Her tight Afro crop-top made me think of a marine, which was at odds with her obvious pregnancy. Amazing cheekbones highlighted cocoa-golden eyes.

"I swear, paper breeds like rabbits." She shook my hand as I sat down across from her. "I hate paperwork."

Tamar sighed. "It's necessary."

"I know, but I hate it."

Tamar put her hand on my shoulder. "I couldn't talk Amanda into staying. Maybe you'll have better luck."

I gave Tamar a sour look. "I doubt anyone can

change my mind. I have a lot of unfinished business. Sharon sort of interrupted it."

"I hear that," J. T. said. She shifted in her chair the same way Rosa had, trying to find a position that was remotely comfortable. "Tamar doesn't know how to take no for an answer."

Tamar made a pffting noise and left us alone.

"I've only been back a few hours. Tamar and I have been talking about what we're lacking, and it seemed like you might be the right balance. But actually, she told me more about Sharon than you."

That was just Tamar's worldview of what was really important. "There's not much to tell. Sharon just dropped into my life. That's the only reason I'm here."

"But you helped her out when it must have been terrifying."

I felt like a model of courage. The warm fuzzies around here definitely came from J. T. "I pretty much freaked out."

"Yeah, I know what you mean." Those amazing eyes radiated compassion. "I was plenty freaked when Sirena jumped into my dreams. But I'm sure that Sharon told you all about that."

She hadn't, and I didn't know why. "Not much."

"Oh." J. T. pursed her lips thoughtfully for a moment. "Well, Tamar had the idea that you might want to stay, and she's right. We do need someone who can keep us on this planet, if you know what I mean. She may look like the picture of practicality, but her orbit is just as high as mine."

"I can believe that. She is a doer with big dreams."

"That's Tamar. If it hadn't been for her, I would have been happy to open a free clinic and let everyone walk right in. She made me see that while that would definitely help maybe hundreds of people a day, it wouldn't change anything. People would still shoot and knife each other and think why not — we'll get healed."

I was confused. "Are you a healer like Sharon is?"

J. T. blinked. "Didn't anyone tell you?"

I shook my head. "I haven't exactly made myself available for orientation. I had a lot to think about."

"Well, Sirena gave those of us who helped her gifts. I was a nurse before Sirena came along. I was trying to bring some healing and peace into an increasingly violent world. I'd never had the money to go to medical school, and the more I saw of the way some doctors treated people the less I wanted to be one. I just wanted to make people feel better."

"I can understand that. Making it better — it's one of the things that women can be very good at."

J. T. smiled as if I was a gifted and perceptive person. My self-esteem went up two notches. I was willing to bet she had that effect on everyone. "Then Sirena came along. She showed me there was more than here and now. I haven't exactly been willing to go to a lab and find out how she did give me this healing gift. We're thinking of opening a biomedical lab, because if everybody could do it, well, I have to think that some people would stop killing as a way to feel important. Anyway, Sirena gave it to me, and I am passing it on to my children. Two boys so far and this" — she patted her stomach — "is a girl."

It would have been hard to take in if I hadn't

spent the last week surrounded by women who occasionally brushed my thoughts and believed that Pallas existed. "So your healing is paying for this place?"

J. T. looked a little sad. "I didn't want it that way, but it made too much sense. When my kids are grown maybe I'll get to open that free clinic, but now preserving and passing on the talent is the single best thing I can do. And I can bring money in here, very quietly, and not attract a lot of attention."

"You'd be overrun." There was no way one woman could meet all the inevitable demand for a healer like her.

"After what we went through extracting ourselves from the police when Sirena was here, the last thing we wanted was attention. For the sake of all our children, for Gallina, too."

"Are all the children here . . . special?"

"Yes, of course. Ask their parents." J. T. grinned.

"You know what I mean."

Her grin softened. "Sirena gave us belief in ourselves. There were five of us. We've all given that belief to many others. Some women come here to keep it in their daily lives. The children who don't believe in themselves soon begin to. If I didn't already believe in miracles, I would now. It's a miracle these days if children believe in themselves, and they keep on believing while they grow into young men and women who teach their lovers and friends to believe in themselves. That kind of confidence can remake the world."

"You won't get any argument from me." If I'd believed in myself a little more, I might have stayed in Washington, stayed with Laney and tried to make up for what I'd done there. Instead, I ran. I ran because I didn't believe I could ever atone for my mistake. If I'd started atoning then, working selflessly to help others, I might have reached a point where I thought the scales had leveled. Now all I had left was a desperate plan that would surely fail.

"It's my favorite theme," J. T. admitted. "Do you believe in miracles?"

It was a deceptively simple question. "If you mean fishes into loaves and water into wine, praise Jesus, I'm afraid not. My grandfather was a Baptist preacher — he tried, and I still didn't believe."

"I had a preacher uncle, but it was my mother who convinced me. When I told her I wasn't going to church any more because it was a lot of nonsense — I think I was a smart-aleck twelve or thirteen — she asked me why I didn't believe in miracles. I said I'd never seen one. So she performed one for me."

I had to smile. "How did she do that?"

"She asked me if I thought it was possible for stars to come inside our house. I said no, of course, and she smacked me upside my head so hard that I saw stars right there in our living room."

I was both horrified and amused. "I hope she didn't do that often."

"No, not often. Only when she wanted me to remember something very important and I was being deliberately ignorant. I've never forgotten — miracles can and do happen anywhere and everywhere. We just have to see them. Hopefully, without being smacked upside the head first."

I chuckled. "I think I could have used a smack or two at just the right time."

J. T. rubbed her crop-top absentmindedly. "Healing for money wasn't what I wanted, but once we started to conceive of this place and what we might be able to do — the vision was so big and so worthwhile that I had to support it. I also had only a few years left to make babies — until Sirena said it, I didn't think there was a good reason to bring another baby into this world. She gave me a reason and a belief that I could help make a world worthy of my children. I had to save a lot of energy for that. So I went where there was money and a lot of it. Wealthy people with nerve injuries for the most part."

"Can you cure conditions like cancer?"

She shook her head. "No, I can only make whole what is broken. Do you remember that tennis player who had the spinal cord injury from the car accident? They said he'd never walk again?"

It was my turn to shake my head. "I don't follow the news much. Well, not at all, really."

"That makes you hard to impress and shows me I'm too full of myself. Well, he and others like him built this place."

I tapped my lips with my spoon. "So the wealthy get all the healthcare they want —"

"While the poor don't, I know. But give us fifteen more years and we'll change all that." J. T. had made peace with necessity, but it was only temporary. "We're making a miracle here. It's not retro or separatist or back-to-anything. It's a simple belief in human potential. It took an alien to make us see that we can be better human beings."

I wasn't in a position to know if they were going to succeed with their dream. They'd made a good start, better than most well-meaning groups. J. T. and Tamar were thinking generationally, trying to change the world by growing better people. I wanted them to succeed.

J. T. would have said more, but Tamar arrived with Sharon. "I managed to tear her away from Gallina, finally."

J. T. rose to embrace her, then sighed. "I can feel it all over you — the energy that Sirena had. Thank you so much for taking such a big chance. Gallina needed you."

"I needed to come as much as she needed me. I've gained more than I've given." Sharon sat down in the other chair.

Tamar lounged against the wall. "I tried not to worry about her isolation, but I did. When I figured out she was using telepathy, I knew how easy it would be for her to grow up manipulating people. How could I teach her right and wrong in matters I knew almost nothing about?"

J. T. took Tamar's hand. "It's really Sirena? She really made it? And Maddy?"

"They both made it." The two women shared a small sigh, as if the bond of memory was intimate, then Tamar untangled her fingers from J. T.'s with a touch of sheepishness I would have thought impossible for her to ever feel.

J. T. asked Sharon a lot of the questions I'd asked her about what Pallas was like, then if Sirena would approve of what they were doing with her gift. I tuned it out because J. T. had given me so much to think about.

I came back to the conversation when I realized that all three women were looking at me expectantly.

"Well," Sharon persisted. "Do you?"

"I'm sorry, do I what?"

"Want to go for a walk?"

"Oh." I grinned sheepishly. "Of course. I was just thinking about getting smacked upside the head."

J. T. laughed and said she hoped we would stay for a while longer.

"You're far away," Sharon said. Our footsteps crunched on the gravel walk that led from the community building toward our guest quarters.

"I'm just thinking about what J. T. said. Darn — I meant to ask her something else." I hesitated.

"What's the question? Maybe I know the answer."

We paused on a footbridge that spanned a small creek. The sound of running water made me feel this could be home. It would be easy to stay. I was still suspicious of easy solutions and too much comfort I hadn't earned.

"She said the Gardens was not about separatism, but I don't see any men."

"Not so far. From what I've seen, it's pretty clear there was a reason that only lesbians could hear Sirena. Maybe they're attuned to a particular female wavelength — I don't know. When they started to tell friends and old lovers about their dreams, lesbians were the first to believe." She put her back to the railing and looked steadily at me. "Not everybody here is a lesbian, though. Tamar isn't. But she learned to tune in. Everyone — everyone who comes here learns to tune in."

"Tune in to what?"

"Their hearts. The hearts of others. They learn to be sensitive to the hearts of others and to listen clearly to what their own heart is telling them and what their world is urging them to do."

"I think that has happened to me." I looked past her into the darkness. "I know what my heart wants, more than anything."

Sharon asked faintly, "What?" She had never looked more vulnerable than when she waited for my answer.

"To stay here with you."

Sharon's jaw trembled. "Me, too."

We listened to the water for a minute, then she took my hand. Her touch was full of heartbreak.

I finally said it. "Then why do we both know we can't?"

11

She was like water and silk against me. We both accepted that something was coming to an end, and we made love with more tenderness than ever before.

:You said you wouldn't break my heart.:

I kissed her nose and chin. "I said I would try — just something else I failed at."

"Don't do that." She nibbled my shoulder. "Don't think you've failed me."

"I don't want you to go back."

"I know. I don't want to leave you. Sometimes I

feel like my head isn't my own. When I'm with you I know I can find the strength to stay and adapt and grow and not fuck it up so much. But then I work with Sela and Gallina and I miss — I miss home and the community that raised me. I wouldn't be going back to confinement. I'd be one of them. Well, almost." In the dim light I could see her dashing away tears. "I don't know if I'd almost be one of them more than I would almost be one of you. I don't know where I belong anymore."

The familiar ache threatened to overwhelm me. "I want to stay here, but I have a life I never led. Hosteen Sam isn't well, you know —"

"I know."

"I want to be there for him. I wasn't there for my grandparents when their time came. He never married and though he has been singer for many people and has had many students, I feel like he's my only family." My voice was hoarse with tears. "Something he said makes me think he loved my grandmother and that's why he was always there for me. I spent thirteen years feeling sorry for myself and never visiting. I thought that shutting myself away would keep me from hurting anyone else, and I squandered all that love. Laney, and Hosteen Sam, and people like Tommy and Rosa. All that love waiting for me, and I never showed up to take it."

She cradled my hand against her wet cheek. "When I'm gone you should find Laney. You never know what could happen."

"Don't say that. I don't want to find someone else."

She used my finger to trace her forehead. "Two

very lonely people spent a lot of time together, and what happened was not unexpected. Any two people would have —"

"Stop it." I knew I was the one who had said that neither of us was emotionally in a position to judge our feelings. We were both too inexperienced and, as she said, too lonely. I didn't want to hear that right now.

"What would you rather I said?" She pulled out of my arms and snuggled into one of the pillows.

I was scared and telling myself that I had given up too many chances for love already. "I'm in love with you, all of you, especially the part of you that makes mistakes."

She cried into the pillow. I'd finally said what I meant. It wasn't fair that it was breaking both our hearts.

She finally blew her nose. "I keep being recognized. We should have realized that because of what I am and who I was coming to see that I would naturally come into contact with people who have been involved with or are very interested in the space program. They've all seen her picture. Even with the hair change they recognize me. They seem to believe me when I say it's just a resemblance. But the doubt is there. They look at me and think something's not quite right. While it's okay for Tamar and Gallina and J. T. and their closest circle to know the truth, the more people who know or suspect, the more likely it is outsiders will find out —"

"And the villagers will arrive with pitchforks."

She sniffed. "You got that right."

I knew she was thinking of me and my tire iron. "There's always a nose job and new cheekbones."

"It's too late for that. If I'd done it right away, then maybe it would have all worked. J. T. and Tamar have worked so hard. I'm a risk they don't need."

"Then leave with me."

"Someone will come looking for me. As much as I love you." She stroked my cheek gently. "As much as I want to stay, I can't live on the run, always looking over my shoulder. If I'm going to be here, I want to live — I want to see everything and be everywhere. If I go back to Pallas, I'll be free to see everything there. It's a world just as diverse and as exciting as this one."

"But there's no me." It was my last card to play, and I knew it wasn't a winning one.

"Every paradise has a flaw," she said softly. "Free to be myself and heartbroken? I have to think that's better than having a whole heart and living a lie."

"It's not fair that you have to make a choice like that."

"I don't feel mature enough to make the choice. I can't let anyone else do it for me, though."

I wanted to argue more, but I accepted that I would not change her mind. We hadn't talked about my plans, and I knew I would not change my mind either. Her certainty only made me more certain. "How do you get home?"

She sighed. "I have to get to someplace fairly remote and wait for a storm. Do you remember what I said about how we travel?"

I'd thought about little else. "I thought you just hopped on to one of those time threads." I was very interested in her answer.

"I'm not strong enough to do it that way, not for the distance I must travel. Sela will send me the extra power. Storms actually augment the whole effect — that's how I ended up in the wrong place. I had more power than I knew how to handle, and I forgot where I was going for a second."

"I'll help you," I said. I must have accepted it too easily, because I felt the quick brush of her mind.

"Amy," she breathed. "You can't do what you're planning."

Damn. Well, better to argue about it now. "I don't see why not."

"Because time doesn't work that way. You can't go back and change something you did."

"You did it twice."

"A matter of minutes and affecting very few physical placements. I know I explained it badly, but that's what I know."

"The past creates the future. There were a lot of futures destroyed by what I did."

"The future exists regardless of the past. The universe marches forward without our help."

I just couldn't believe that. It seemed to me that there was an enduring and very human yearning to start over at least once. Even Tamar and J. T. would do things differently if they could start over. "Maybe you're wrong. You've been wrong before."

"What if you're right, then? What if you can change the past and let another future happen? Will I still exist? Will this place exist? How can you justify destroying what already is for the sake of redeeming your personal mistake?"

I hadn't thought of that. I was convinced that if I could somehow stop myself from sending the facsimile, that everything would go back to being the way it ought to have been. I would be what I should have been. The future would be what it should have been. Sirena would still get lost and Tamar and J. T. would still build this place. All that was good would still exist in what had to be a better future.

But what about Sharon? She would not exist in a future where the *Challenger* did not explode. If all the science fiction writers I'd ever read were correct, I would never remember her because she had never been created. Her existence was what had given me the courage to break out of the past and now to actually change it. My mistake had given me the means to fix my mistake.

I reasoned in circles and came no closer to answers.

What I knew was that I felt the love in her touch and it was profound. She had marked my spirit. Could I give that up and not know something was missing? Wouldn't I feel the emptiness?

She continued persuasively, "Either I'm right or you're right. Either way, you don't get what you want."

"I'm not going to get what I want any way. So why not try?" There was a third way — we were both right. We might both be right.

"I can't help you. I won't help you. I do have some guiding ethics."

There was no point to arguing further, so I kissed her, knowing there was now a finite number of times that I could do so. The whisper of her breath against my cheek was as arousing as the brush of her fingers along my forearms.

Passion was healing, but it also burned. Loving her, wanting her, had healed much of my aching soul. Losing her was another blow. No matter what

happened I was going to lose her, but I could not
believe that I would not know what she had meant to
me. I would remember that she loved me. It would be
more than I'd had before. It could be a reason to go
on.

We lingered for a few days more, then it became
unbearable for both of us. I was even more greatly
tempted to stay, but I was also having the same
nightmares I'd had just after the shuttle accident.

Sharon discovered that in spite of her denials,
someone had taken a picture of her and compared it
on a computer to one of Christa McAuliffe. Wild
speculation circulated that the Pallasians had saved
McAuliffe as a gift of some sort. Sooner or later
someone would put the two pictures on the Internet,
and the conspiracy nuts would come sniffing at the
gates.

Tamar and J. T. were not sure that they could
quell the rumor. They'd worked hard to keep the
women who believed in the Pallasians from thinking
the Pallasians were godlike in their wisdom and
powers. Like Sharon had told me at the very
beginning, we were too willing to believe in great
spacefaring races who obeyed ethical directives and
had only our best interests at heart.

We had to go. One night, after most people were
asleep, we just slipped away. I don't think I had ever
done anything that hard in my life. Sharon was with
me, and that made it harder still. I knew we could
not end this journey together. It was a journey to an

ending. If I got my wish for a new beginning there would be no her, and who knew what else would change?

Every time I woke up in a sweat, with the patterns of those twin plumes of exhaust seared into my vision, I knew more certainly that the injustice of it had to be fixed. They hadn't been meant to die. When they survived, whatever that different future was had to be better for their being in it. They were that kind of people. Sharon Christa McAuliffe had been that kind of person. Because of me, she hadn't had a chance to finish her work.

We retraced our journey home. Why not, Sharon had said. I would know when a storm was coming. We could stay close until then.

I couldn't go back to the hogan, that much I knew. I would sometimes visit to reclaim the peacefulness of it, but I couldn't live with that much solitude for long. Edna Beaker offered us the run of her house while I tried to find a way to settle into life in Chinle.

I wondered how much of my charade Sharon believed. I made all the right sounds and motions to imply I was indeed settling down. But I was just waiting for a storm.

I was changing little Hana's diaper when I felt the air shift. Rosa's newest daughter had a lusty cry, and she seemed to prefer Aunt Amanda's company second only to Mom. Mom did have the endless milk supply.

I had left Sharon with Hosteen Sam for the day. She wanted to learn a little bit of Blessing Way song to take home with her. We'd never explained to him just where Sharon's home was. He'd never asked either.

Rosa agreed with me a storm was on the way and said she understood that I had to go. She had no idea how far. I felt guilty that I couldn't tell her, but the story was too long and too incredible.

Sharon was waiting for me when I arrived at Hosteen Sam's.

"I told him I had to leave when the weather turned. He never asked why, but he said it was turning today."

"It is," I said. I took my time kissing her. "We should go soon."

"Little Red," Hosteen Sam called, "are you going to stand on my porch all day?"

I went inside and, as I had so often, found him stitching feathers to a ceremonial mask. His thick gray braids were dotted with bits of down. "I have to take Sharon away." I sat down with my knees near his.

"She has to go home. I understand. Even eagle longs for her nest."

"It's a long way. I'll very likely never see her again."

"I am sad for you, Little Red. Don't let your sadness hold her back. It's a long way to the stars."

It took a moment for his words to sink in. I finally said, "How did you know?"

"That is an interesting story I would like to tell you. You don't have time to hear it all now. First Man and First Woman made this world beautiful. Why would they stop here? Maybe this world was not their

188

first effort. Maybe they started someplace else and found the Uglyway. Maybe First Man and First Woman came here to start over."

I blinked back tears of guilt and relief. "Is there any situation you cannot cover with a Navajo story? You were right about her being my Happiness Girl. We made Changing Woman together. She's going home and it's just an extension of First Man and First Woman's love for the people."

His fingers returned to stitching. "Wind is flexible. When wind is confronted by rock, it bends around rock. Belief must be flexible or you will never wear the rock away."

I knew that Sharon was listening, and I also knew she was crying. We'd held in our tears these last few days, but now they had to fall. "I might not come back, either."

His gray-brown gaze flicked to my face. "It is right for you to go with Happiness Girl."

Sharon tensed, as if afraid of what I would say.

"I can't go with her. But there is something I have to try. I don't know if she will help me. But I'm still going to try. If I don't come back, I want you to put this letter in the mail. Will you do that for me?"

"I will do as you ask. I hope I do not have to, Little Red."

I kissed him on his weathered cheek. As I closed the door I heard him begin to sing Blessing Way. It was the part where Born for Water passes his father's tests and clears the way for the people to live safely in the world.

I drove us past all the tourist overlooks, past

Spider Rock, and even past the access road that wound down to where the hogan was. We finally stopped where a lone and scraggly cottonwood marked the end of the road. The cliffs here were sloped and rounded, and it would be easier to watch the storm's approach.

Sharon walked quickly to the view while I parked the Jeep under the tree. I left the keys in it. When Sharon wasn't looking I tucked a small pouch into a nook in the tree. The letter Hosteen Sam had would tell Tamar where to find it.

Sharon had said it was quite simple. She would signal Sela when she was ready, and that would be that.

We stood at cliff's edge with the wind whipping our hair. A towering accumulation of thunderclouds was funneling around New Mexico's mountains and bringing chaos to the canyon below.

"You can come with me," Sharon blurted out.

"What?" I didn't, couldn't understand.

"I didn't tell you about Sirena and how she made it home because I didn't want you to know. You have too much to keep you here."

I stared at her. "Couldn't you let me decide for myself?"

"I was afraid I'd talk you into it."

We were both so afraid of happiness neither of us felt we deserved and so suspicious of what would be too easy. "I can't go with you." I had to raise my voice a little as the wind grew louder. "You were right. I have too much here. And you know what I want to do, if you'll just help me."

"It won't work, Amy."

"Show me how to try. Let me at least try."

The hiss of rain was coming closer. The sandstone was warm from the sun earlier in the day, and it drank the rain greedily.

Sharon turned to face the spectacle. I almost didn't hear her words. "What if it meant I wouldn't exist? Could you really do that?"

I put my arms around her from behind and felt all her anguish. :*I know that could happen.*:

:*Would you do it?*:

I turned her to face me. "You're the one who told me the future doesn't need the past to exist."

"Then what do you hope to change?"

"I want to change the bad. I want to be free to accept what's good and not question if I have the right to happiness."

Lightning flickered in the distance, and the first raindrops spattered on us. What she said was lost in the low rumble of thunder.

"Say that again," I urged.

"You don't need my help."

"I can't find those threads without you." There was another flash of lightning, much closer. It was only three seconds until thunder made itself heard.

"You have your own thread, Amy. You always have had it. All that you have learned from me should let you see it and use it. Close your eyes . . ."

The curtain of rain enveloped us. It ran down my face like tears. She held me tight while I closed my eyes, trying to find a different way of looking. Nothing seemed any different. I was being rained on and she was going away — these thoughts distracted me.

:*Sharon, it's time.*: Sela was suddenly there in my thoughts.

Sharon's lips were on mine. *:I will never forget you, no matter what. I will always love you.:*

I saw her thoughts come to me. They were like fireflies, gently illuminating what I could only see as darkness. The darkness faded, and a bright flash of lightning showed me Sharon and the thread that ran up from the earth and through her to the heavens. She let go of me and stepped back.

:Look at yourself, Amy. You've always been where you are. Changing the past won't change you.:

I looked down to see my own thread more tangible than my own body. I could put my hands around it. *:I see it, I see it now!:*

She didn't answer. I looked up to see her wrapping her arms hard around herself, and then I heard a sound like an avalanche or an earthquake.

She was gone.

Tears escaped from my tightly closed eyes. There was another flash of lightning and I could still see my own thread in the ultra white glare. I doubted that I would be able to enter this state without her. I didn't have time to grieve. My world without her did not seem worth preserving. I wondered if I could go back to the day we met and live it again just to watch her move and hear her voice.

Suddenly that was where I was. I watched her fall off the boulder into the water. I surfed along the events until I was inside what the past remembered of me. I *did* knock her back into the water. I *did* break my leg. Damn. She healed me and then I was in the water again. This time I didn't knock her back in and I didn't break my leg.

I gripped my thread lifeline and formed my resolve. I thought deliberately and specifically about the moment I had stood in front of the facsimile machine.

Then I was there.

I tried as hard as I could to be inside of who I had been. I tried to make myself realize that what I was doing was wrong. It wasn't working. I was trying too hard. There had to be something simpler.

I forgot about trying to tell myself anything. I concentrated on my hands. I could feel my hands in the past, like ghosts, sliding the paper into the send tray. It took all my concentration to keep in contact.

Abruptly, I had a horrible sensation of falling, for just a moment, and I grappled for the thread. I had almost let go, and my instinct told me that letting go would be a very bad mistake.

I tried to divide my mind. Part to keep a firm grip on the thread and part to control the past me. I strained again, felt the beginnings of a terrible headache, and then the difference between me and the past me was gone. For the time it took to turn the memorandum over so that the scanner would have only a blank page to send, I was who I had been. I pressed Start, and NASA Administration received an empty page. If someone called to ask about it, all the past me would know was that it had been an honest mistake for someone using a fairly new piece of equipment.

It was done.

I slipped back to my veiled awareness. I was weak

and pleased. For a moment, I didn't know what to do next, then I realized I had to see the launch. I had to forever erase the memory of the white plume of exhaust forking into two explosions. I had lived with that image for too long.

I thought about that day, then I was there. Tuesday, January 28, 1986. I chatted with people and ran papers to the Capitol and hoped to run into Laney. I watched my innocent self and wondered when things would begin to change. I was at my desk when Tom came out of his office. This is it, I thought. The launch is scrubbed.

"Challenger is a go," Tom announced. It was almost eleven-thirty. "I just heard from a buddy that the Air and Space Museum is going to show the NASA launch feed on their IMAX system. Anyone want to head down there?"

There I was, excited and eager, hurrying to the theater. I watched myself find a seat and all the while I was numb — how could the launch still be a go? Hadn't not sending the fax been enough? What more could I do?

I was limited to my own thread. Sharon had seemed to have access to several, but I was stuck with my own. I couldn't travel time and space to the launch center and set off an alarm that would halt the launch sequence. I couldn't jump into the orbiter and tell Commander Scobee about the O-rings. I was stuck with my past. It was the only thing I could change.

My past didn't have what it took to change this particular moment in history. What I had done had been wrong, but it obviously had played a very small part in NASA's decision to launch. I should have rejoiced, but instead I felt a vast sense of loss. The universe makes its own future, and to make it these seven people had to die.

Judy Resnik's exuberant "All right" was barely audible as the theater sound system conveyed the booming rumble of the solid fuel boosters igniting.

The launch was going off as scheduled.

They were all doomed, again. I was cheering, again. I lost awareness of the theater for a moment when I fell to my knees in the pouring rain. Holding myself in the past was slowly draining me.

Both of my heartbeats started the countdown. I lifted my gaze to the screen. Ten seconds, twenty, thirty. At forty-nine seconds the wind shear shattered the glassy oxides that had so far contained the explosion and flame reached the liquid fuel tanks. Commander Scobee said he was throttling up. T plus 1:10.

Time is the longest distance between two places. A long, long distance away lightning struck near me and the energy traveled into the breach I was holding open, half there and half in the past, holding tight to the thread of my future while my cry of disbelief echoed through time.

Pieces of the orbiter were scattered across the sky. I reached up as if to catch them as they fell, my hands silhouetted against the giant screen. They were falling to their deaths at two hundred and seven miles per hour and I still would have given anything to save them.

In the stunned silence of the theater I clung to my chair as a wave of sickening vertigo threatened to knock me to the floor. Was it the explosion that cast such a bright light or the remnants of the lightning strike? I heard a roaring sound, like an avalanche or an earthquake.

Time is the shortest distance between two places.

I had lost the thread.

12

Fingers of icy wind found their way into the ancient homes of the Anasazi, and trailed across the river where the People's children had played for millennia. The gravelly shore and picnic tables had long been abandoned for winter. The icy touch of the wind sent jack rabbits scampering into their burrows and a lone kinglet flapping home with the last prey it would catch that day.

I disturbed the kinglet as I walked the trail I had come to know very well. Hosteen Sam had shown it to me long ago when I first asked to spend time at the hogan in between semesters.

I was clinging to the side of the cliff, nearly at the ledge, when my cell phone rang. I knew who it was without checking. With a final surge of energy, I pulled myself onto the ledge and lay there panting while I scrabbled the phone out of my pocket.

I didn't even say hello. "I will call you as soon as I know anything. I promised I would and I will."

Tamar didn't waste time on hellos either. "I was betting you forgot to remind the plastic surgeon."

Damn. I had forgotten. She was going to be insufferable. "Would you do that for me?"

Tamar hung up without another word, but her I-told-you-so came through loud and clear. We'd known each other since just before the birth of her daughter, and we still didn't like each other very much. It kept our working relationship on behalf of the Pallas Foundation strong.

The storm was every bit as magnificent as I remembered. It was a relief, after all these years, to finally have memories mesh with reality.

Reality. I laughed into the wind. I'd wasted almost a lifetime thinking I had done something I had not. I'd given up a future and the love that could redeem me to fix something that hadn't been broken. What did I know about reality?

Sharon had told me the future doesn't rely on the past. Somehow I had been given thirteen years to live over. My memories told me that thirteen years was an interminably long time. The first time around they had never seemed to come to an end. The second time around there were simply not enough hours in the day to get ready for the future.

I wish I had paid more attention to the future when I was there. Important things, like stock prices. That would have been useful. As soon after the tragic launch as I could, I went back to the Canyon, back to the end of the road and the cottonwood tree where I had last seen Sharon.

The Jeep wasn't there. Maybe because it was never hers. But the pouch she had given me, that had come with her through time and space, was still nestled in the cottonwood tree. She had told me to keep the diamonds and use them to help Tamar.

I did just that. I knew enough to invest all that I could in Blue Chip stocks, dump them in September of 1987, and reinvest them again just after Black Monday.

Years later, when I introduced myself to Tamar Reese, I had an amazing bankroll and a proposal to start the Pallas Foundation. She and J. T. were already grappling with possiblities when I walked in with money, land and answers to many of their questions.

If we stood at the dawning of a new reality, when the time would come where we had to choose our future, then we would be ready. Pallas Foundation Centers had been carefully seeded here and abroad, and now they sprung up on their own. All it took was one person, usually a woman, and often a lesbian, to believe she could do it. Her convictions brought others, and they raised walls and sat down to build a better community.

The mother house in the San Gabriel Canyon was largely symbolic. J. T. lived there while I preferred to live in the Center just outside of Window Rock, the tribal seat of the Navajo Nation, and Tamar moved back and forth. An agreeable Tribal Council had been happy to grant the Foundation some land and watch what would grow from their generosity. If their own *hataalii,* the great singer Sam Nakai, said it would be like First Man and First Woman coming again, how could they argue with that? So they watched and waited.

My waiting was almost done. I'd waited through my life again, always doing, always preparing. I'd finished law school and passed the bar and made money and bought land and studied cultures. I'd made friends in low and high places, always looking for open minds that would welcome a community that taught that we were all better than our past.

I'd let myself love Laney, but when loving got in the way of friendship, we'd kept the friendship because it was harder to find. Though we got together for a long time as often as possible, I saw her more frequently on C-SPAN with the word *Congresswoman* under her name.

These latter years, no matter how busy I was, I made a point of visiting in Chinle — Hosteen Sam, Tommy and Rosa, Mrs. Beaker and more. I gave away as much love as I could and learned that it all came back to me.

In another few minutes I would find out if all my planning and all my work had been enough. The rain was drumming toward me, and I welcomed it.

When I had found myself starting over I had no idea what I'd done. If I had caused the future where I loved Sharon and she loved me to go away, why did I remember it? I couldn't remember what hadn't ever happened, could I?

Thunder rumbled from up the canyon and the rain

increased to a roar. White plumes of cloud pierced the high-country blue, and it took me briefly to the second time I lived through the shuttle explosion. I had gotten my wish. I had changed my past. It hadn't changed what I had so hoped it would. Tragedy and injustice exist and life can only flower on a cemetery. Stars died so that all I was and could be, all that I loved and hated, and would ever know, could live.

It was just about time, I judged. I slithered down the cliff, celebrating the rain in my eyes and the icy knife of the wind. I was finally done with the past. Halfway down I paused and waited.

There was a bright flash of silver light, then a sound like an avalanche or an earthquake.

I wasn't so much running as I was dancing. I might have to convince her about the plastic surgery and even to stay here, but if my heart remembered, then so would hers. Time is the shortest distance between two hearts, and we had a brand new future to live.

**Publications from
Bella Books, Inc.**
The best in contemporary lesbian fiction

**P.O. Box 10543, Tallahassee, FL 32302
Phone: 800-729-4992
www.bellabooks.com**

WITHOUT WARNING: Book one in the Shaken series by KG MacGregor. *Without Warning* is the story of their courageous journey through adversity, and their promise of steadfast love.
ISBN: 978-1-59493-120-8
$13.95

THE CANDIDATE by Tracey Richardson. Presidential candidate Jane Kincaid had always expected the road to the White House would exact a high personal toll. She just never knew how high until forced to choose between her heart and her political destiny.
ISBN: 978-1-59493-133-8
$13.95

TALL IN THE SADDLE by Karin Kallmaker, Barbara Johnson, Therese Szymanski and Julia Watts. The playful quartet that penned the acclaimed *Once Upon A Dyke* and *Stake Through the Heart* are back and now turning to the Wild (and Very Hot) West to bring you another collection of erotically charged, action-packed tales.
ISBN: 978-1-59493-106-2
$15.95

IN THE NAME OF THE FATHER by Gerri Hill. In this highly anticipated sequel to *Hunter's Way*, Dallas Homicide Detectives Tori Hunter and Samantha Kennedy investigate the murder of a Catholic priest who is found naked and strangled to death.
ISBN: 978-1-59493-108-6
$13.95